SHIFT WORK

KILHAVEN POLICE 1

BROCK BLOODWORTH
H. CLAIRE TAYLOR

Cover by Damonza

www.damonza.com

FFS Media, LLC

www.ffs.media

contact@ffs.media

CONTENTS

The smoking gun felt like a body part now. It had fused to his hands sometime between when he opened fire and when he heard and felt the first fruitless click of the empty magazine as he rapidly pulled the trigger again and again. The muscles in Officer Green's limbs shook from adrenaline and fatigue as he held his .40 at arm's length, aware of more things at once than he knew was possible for a human brain —the man spread out on the pavement, the *pop-pop-pop-pop* of the other officers' firearms, the burnt smell of gun smoke, every single light source that illuminated the dark and grisly scene, the placement of each squad car and officer, the pulse of blood in his ears, the churning in his gut, even the mountain of paperwork that would be waiting for him because of this. But what he perceived most acutely in this whole slow-motion mess was a simple phrase that ricocheted around his brain like the silver bullets just fired from his department-issued pistol. The phrase felt so pronounced that it seemed to be written in neon lights above the limp body of the suspect, and it was, simply: *Congrats! You're fucked.*

Officer Green waited for the suspect to change form—initial reports said this one was a shifter or were-beast of some type, but the full message hadn't been coherently conveyed from the frantic caller to the telepath dispatcher then back out to officers near the location.

But the suspect didn't change, not even a little bit.

Maybe he wasn't dead.

Or maybe he's not a shifter or were-beast, you idiot.

Green ignored that last thought, realizing that he should check to see if the guy was dead before thinking of worst-case scenarios. And then maybe he should begin life-saving measures if this jerk was still kicking. Nothing had ever seemed more absurd and also more urgent to him than rendering aid to the suspect he'd just plugged with at least a few silver bullets.

Oh shit. What if I missed every shot? What if it was one of the others that hit him?

That possibility was somehow more dreadful than the one where he'd just killed another creature for the first time in his life.

"Stop shooting!" he shouted, although the other officers had already done so by then.

Green approached the suspect quickly but cautiously, his shaky fingers fumbling with the spare magazine as he attempted to reload. But then he felt the magazine strike gold and extended his gun out in front of him.

"You good?" shouted Officer Lawrence, rushing up to his side.

Green didn't dare lift his finger from his pistol for a

second, not even to give a thumbs-up. He nodded exaggeratedly instead. "Yeah, you?"

"All good," Lawrence replied, close on his right now. "Brooks, you good?"

"Yeah, I'm good," she replied. "Weapon's secure."

As he bent down toward the suspect, the smell of evacuated bowels alone should have told him all he needed to know, but he had to be sure, not just for his peace of mind, but because procedure called for it. This situation was fucked enough without him piling policy violations onto the heap.

There was an alarming lack of blood for how many bullet holes were immediately visible. The odd detail lodged itself into Green's mind, even as he reached in his belt for his gloves.

But before he could successfully slip them onto his sweaty fingers, a firm hand on his shoulder caused him to turn. He stared into the clear blue eyes of Officer Heather Valance. Never in his life had he thought he would be relieved to see his nightmare of a former field training officer in all her terrifyingly intense glory.

"Oh hell," Brooks said from somewhere behind Valance, "looks like I'm shot."

As his worst fears bubbled to the surface of his mind, he leaned to the side to see past Valance.

The suspect's gun dangled in one of Brooks's hands, and she looked down at her leg like maybe someone had splashed a little mud on it. "I think I'm OK." She looked up and waved off the other officers. "Just nicked me."

As Officer Lawrence rushed over to her anyway, Valance grabbed Green's shoulders and shook him gently. "Take a deep breath, Officer. Think. What's first?"

He struggled to turn his brain on again. It seemed to have ducked for cover the moment the suspect fired, allowing instinct and training to take over.

He swallowed. "Cuffs." She nodded and let go of his shoulders so he could proceed.

But when he reached down for his silvers, she added, "No point. Irons instead."

Not a good sign. But Green clicked on the iron cuffs anyway before rolling the suspect first to one side to check for more weapons, then over onto his back. The man was dead weight. Green hoped not literally.

Valance placed two ungloved fingers on the suspect's neck, but her calm face already seemed resigned to a particular outcome. She nodded then looked up at Green, and her icy eyes urging him to pay attention. "It was a good shoot. You know it, I know it, and every other officer here knows it. Got that?"

Green swallowed and nodded.

"Let's get this done. Check his pulse."

"Gloves?" Green asked.

"Sure. Fine."

Green slipped one on and checked for a pulse. The suspect seemed very dead. "Nothing," Green croaked.

Valance sighed. "We're not calling it yet. Let the paramedics do that whenever they get their ass over here. What next?"

Green nodded. "Chest compressions." The rhythmic pumping of the dead man's ribs felt almost Zen amidst the commotion of his fellow officers scrambling to secure the scene and radio out updates. He almost didn't want to stop, even though he knew it was a lost cause. Valance stayed by his side as he continued the futile attempt. At least internal investigations couldn't say he hadn't tried. But Valance probably knew that, which was why she walked him through it and made sure he didn't quit.

When Valance left him, he felt panic rising, but he continued the compressions. It was the only thing he knew to do.

She returned a moment later with gauze and began packing the suspect's wounds. The bleeding had started to slow noticeably, though. Green felt the first wave of exhaustion wash over him a moment before Valance placed a hand on his back, saying, "Green, paramedics are here."

"Huh?" He looked up to see two serious-faced paramedics staring down at him. "Oh." He jumped up to clear the way and stumbled a few steps back, his eyes still glued to the body. "Why didn't he change back?" he asked.

His former FTO didn't answer him, instead leading him toward Officer Brooks's car further down the street from the scene.

Officer Lawrence met them halfway, and Green was vaguely aware that he was being handed off from one babysitter to another.

Didn't matter. Maybe Lawrence would answer his question. "Why didn't he change back?"

Jeremy Lawrence had a blood smear along his handsome, defined jawline, and his usual confident smirk was nowhere to be found. "'Cause he's not a shifter or a were, Green."

Fuck. "What is he?"

"Damn, Green." Lawrence rubbed his hand over his chin, unknowingly smearing the blood around, as he led Green down to the car where Brooks was already being bandaged up by another paramedic. "Thought you'd at least recognize your own kind. That stupid son of a bitch is a human."

"I shot a—? I *killed* another human?"

"Assuming the paramedics call it, yeah. Looks like it," Officer Lawrence added unhelpfully. "If it makes you feel any better, it wasn't just you. Brooks and I got a few rounds in." Lawrence grimaced. "It was a good shoot, Green, alright?"

Officer Green nodded but struggled to breathe with any regularity as he turned to look back at the body.

Lawrence grabbed him and turned him back around, giving him a gentle shove down the hill.

He'd shot a human. He'd *killed* a human. Did it matter that Green was a human, too? *Probably not. Shit.*

Only two months on the job and Green had already screwed his career. Forget about the way people back home were going to treat him now that he'd killed one of his own. Was his whole life fucked because this dumb sieve of a man lying on the ground in front of him just *had* to draw a gun?

His heart pumped rapidly somewhere near his ears as the first glimmer of sunlight peeked in the east, and he suspected this would be the longest morning of his very brief career.

CHAPTER ONE_

EIGHT WEEKS EARLIER.

"You're up, Rookie." Officer Valance chuckled to herself from the driver's seat and pointed lazily toward the disheveled man lying on the sidewalk, illuminated by the headlights of the cruiser.

From where he sat shotgun, Norman Green—Officer Norman Green as of graduating the academy two days ago—gulped and gaped but didn't immediately move. "You think he's dead?"

Officer Valance shrugged and jabbed at the dashboard-mounted Human-Accessible Monitor like she was going for its pressure points. "Hell if I know. He sure looks dead, doesn't he?"

Green nodded. But now wasn't the time to get finicky about touching his first dead body. He unbuckled and slowly opened the car door, knowing he should stop slumping if he was going to give off the proper presence they'd learned in the academy. Presence to whom, though? If this guy was even alive to begin with, he was unconscious.

Presence to the terrifying woman in the car who's in charge of filling out my daily evaluations for the next six weeks.

Green paused a few feet shy of the rigid transient. The man was on his back, his arms and legs sticking straight into the air like a dead raccoon. And what Green wouldn't give to make this magically become a simple dead raccoon. At least it might smell better.

"You poke him yet?" Valance asked.

Green looked up to see his field training officer standing next to the hood of the cruiser, hands clasped together at sternum level. Her espresso hair was pulled back in a tight knot and slicked down by who knew how many layers of gel, leaving Green wondering how often she'd considered shaving it all off since she seemed so confident in her head shape. If he were her, he would just shave his head. Less maintenance. Plus, a shaved head would match her personality even better than a tight bun did.

"Poke him?" Green echoed.

Valance's startlingly blue eyes didn't blink. "Yeah. You poke him? Not with your hands, obviously, but your boot or your nightstick."

"No. I haven't *poked* him." Was she fucking with him?

"Well then." Valance nodded. "Go on." She shifted her weight slightly to get comfortable for the show, and her lean, muscular frame cut an intimidating silhouette against the backdrop of the overwhelmingly bright lights of the gas station behind her.

Green inched forward. Poking the transient with his boot was probably subtler, but if he used his nightstick and the man attacked, he would already be armed.

But Jesus. Did he really want to use a nightstick on his first full night on the job? He'd rather shoot a man than endure the sickening crack of a shin splitting in two from blunt force.

He decided to use his boot, mostly because it didn't require that he lean forward and risk getting a whiff that he might never be able to scrub from his nostrils. Or worse, from his memory. Wasn't smell the most potent sense of memory? If that was the case, he already knew he'd remember his time in Fang sector, which he now called home, vividly until his dying day.

The entire sector smelled faintly like spoiled milk, sulfur, and burnt hair. And Green hadn't even been out to the tiny corner of swampland yet. He could only imagine what new smells that place might hold, because if there was one thing he knew about smells, it was that adding moisture never made them *more* pleasant.

He toed the transient in the bum, which was a mistake for a couple of reasons.

Firstly, there was the wet squishing sound, which could only mean one thing.

Secondly, Valance said, "They teach you that in the academy? Hell. I need to get up to speed with all the latest best practices. I would never have guessed kicking a shifter's shit-filled pants was the way to go."

"How do you know he's a shifter?" Green asked.

"Well, for one, this is typical shifter bullshit. Can't hold his liquor because he's drinking mouthwash. But mostly, this is how shifters pass out. Legs in the air like goddamn roadkill." She glanced away from the body to smirk at Green. "Bet they don't teach you *that* in the academy."

Green shook his head slowly.

Valance huffed. "Of course not. People might find it offensive to point out the obvious differences between creatures. They tiptoe around reality and send us starry-eyed rookies like you who can't even identify a passed out alcoholic shifter when he sees one." Then she added, "Not your fault, though. That's what field training is for, I guess. Go on then. Wake him up."

Knowing the shifter probably wasn't dead helped a little, and as Green leaned forward, mouth breathing as he went, he did notice a slight rise and fall of the man's chest. To avoid leaning any closer to the bulk of the stench, Green grabbed one of the transient's elevated wrists jutting skyward and shook it gently. "Sir!" he yelled.

The shifter didn't stir.

Green shook him harder. "Sir! Are you okay, sir?"

It took a series of progressively rougher kicks to the hip before there was any result.

The shifter jolted awake, his eyes springing open and his body flipping lithely over onto his hands and knees before Green could even register what was happening. "Wha—where—" the shifter yelled, then he promptly vomited on Green's boots.

"Oh Christ," Green said, trying to jump out of the way before another wave of putrescence could slosh up onto the hem of his starched pants, but the movement only managed to fling the puke back into the shifter's face. That ... wasn't ideal.

"Kilhaven Police. Are you okay, sir?"

After another impressively productive heave, the shifter stumbled onto his feet, using a nearby signpost to balance himself. "Brutality!" he yelled. "Police brutality!" He addressed Valance then. "You saw it, right?"

Green turned frantically toward his FTO, wondering if maybe he *had* crossed a line and kicked the man too hard. But his fears were alleviated when he saw the satisfied amusement on Valance's face. "He should have kicked you harder." Then to Green: "You gonna pat him down, or are you in the mood to get shanked by a rusty blade?"

"Huh?" Then it registered, and he quickly refocused on the transient, who was staring at him like he might just take Valance's warning as a suggestion. Green lunged at the shifter, grabbing his wrists—just in the nick of time, it turned out, as Green's sudden movement had startled the drunk, causing him to lurch backward so that he would have fallen, had Green not gotten such a good grasp and hauled him back onto his feet.

He clicked on the handcuffs, and only as the shifter began howling in pain did Green wonder if he'd practice unjustified use of force by selecting the pair of cuffs he had.

"Silver, man? Not cool, not cool," groaned the transient.

But before Green could decide if the steel cuffs would have been a better option, Valance barked, "Quit your whining. You just want in the other pair so your drunk ass can shift into a bird or some shit and escape. Green, the silvers are fine till we pat him down."

Green nodded and started to get his head about him again. "What's your name?"

"B-Rat," the shifter supplied.

"B-Rat?"

"Did I stutter?" B-Rat turned to look over his shoulder at Green. "You look fresh as hell, but I ain't never seen no one grab the silvers bare handed without flinching. What's your deal?"

Before Green could respond, Valance chimed in. "He's

human, you dumbfuck. Jesus, can you not smell it on him? Is your own stank so strong that you can't smell a human when he's standing right next to you?"

B-Rat tried to spin around to get a better look at Green through crossed eyes, but Green surprised even himself with his reaction time and didn't let the shifter turn on him, instead shoving the off-balance man forward, pressing his top half down against the hood of the car.

"Brutality!" cried B-Rat.

"For fuck's sake," Valance said. She reached into her belt and pulled out her rubber gloves, and only then did Green realize he'd been handling the suspect without any protection whatsoever. "You're just upset that you let a human get the best of you. Get used to it. Times, they are a-changing, and the great Kilhaven Police Department is no different. *Diversity matters* and all that." She pressed B-Rat's head to the car to hold him in place then nodded casually at Green. "I suggest you glove up before the pat down."

"Why bother at this point?" Green muttered self-deprecatingly.

Valance's calm, dry amusement transitioned rapidly to humorless alarm. "Uh, you think shit-balloon pants and contact with open sores is the worst of it? Let me tell you something, Officer Green. It can always get grosser. And when you think you've finally found the bottom of the well of grossness, that's exactly when the earth will give way beneath you and you'll fall into a sinkhole of filth the mind can't even comprehend."

"You're hurting me! Brutality!" B-Rat wriggled underneath Valance's palm.

"Shut up. You're fine." She returned her attention to Green like it'd never left. "And even when you're knee-deep in the filth, your brain won't be able to register it. Not right then. But later, sometime, in the dead of night, the sheer grotesqueness you've experienced will finally sink in. You'll wake up in a cold sweat. Maybe you'll have pissed yourself. But compared to the realization that woke you, even your piss will seem like an antibacterial frolic in the spring-fed fountain of youth. You starting to get it?"

"No."

"Good. You couldn't possibly. Now glove up and pat him down. And be sure to check the crotch. They bank on your skittishness. The last thing you want is to end up with your throat slit by a rusty blade because you were too cowardly to firmly grab another man's balls."

Is that really the last *thing I want?* wondered Green as he leaned forward. It was certainly among a long list of things he didn't want.

"That all you got?" B-Rat slurred once Green had gloved up and mustered the courage to suppress his gag reflex long enough to cup the shifter's balls through his crusted pants. "My third wife could grip me firmer than that, and she had the sugar diabetes and could hardly bend her fingers."

"Shut up, scumlicker," Valance growled, and Green wondered if his FTO got in trouble often for the things she said on the job. Maybe no one ever actually reviewed the recordings from their body mics. Chief Spinner certainly wouldn't want something so creaturist to be leaked to the public. As Green learned in the academy, Kilhaven PD was fighting an uphill battle to overcome a history of creaturist incidents and restore its good standing with the public.

Although, the part of Green that grew up biracial in a human town where that sort of thing mattered—unlike Kilhaven, where the main strike against him was that he was human, not that he was dark-skinned—appreciated the break from racism, even if it meant creaturism filled that void in society.

Well, he supposed, people are always going to find something to hate about others.

Valance gazed down at Green where he knelt to check B-Rat's boots for weapons. "He's right," she said. "You gotta get in there, Green."

"I did!" Green protested. "You want me to do a cavity search, too?"

"Only if there's no extra charge," said B-Rat.

Green held his tongue and shook his head but completed the search. "Nothing."

"Hm." Valance pressed her lips into a thin line. "Hold him here." She nodded down toward where her palm was still flat against the side of the shifter's head, pressing it to the cold metal hood. When Green did, probably not holding him as firmly as Valance would like but more firmly than seemed legal, Valance stepped behind the suspect and grabbed a handful of testicles. B-Rat yelped, and Green found himself feeling sorry for the poor drunk.

That is, until Valance said, "Umm-hmm. Just like I thought," and shut her eyes momentarily, as if saying a silent prayer or seeking some higher level of existence before grabbing the waistband of B-Rat's pants, reaching in a gloved hand, and pulling out what appeared to be a photo ID.

Green laughed darkly. "What, no wallet?" But when Valance flicked her wrist and a sharp blade extended out from the ID card, Green's laughter died in his throat. "Oh shit."

"Literally," Valance said casually, flicking a small

something off the card, her upper lip curling only the slightest bit. She grabbed the chain of the cuffs and lifted B-Rat off the hood. "Okay, Boris, you're coming downtown now."

"Boris?" Green asked. "You know this guy?"

Valance didn't pause as she shoved the shifter toward the backseat of the car. "Of course. Does this look like a first-time offender to you? Nah, we have a few warrants out on him. B&E, jerking off within view of a playground—"

"Seriously?" said Green.

"In my defense," B-Rat began, "those children didn't have to look. It wasn't about them."

"Just shut the fuck up, Boris," Valance said. "I mean, *'You have the right to shut the fuck up.'*"

"Oh!" Green said, just before Valance crammed the shifter into the backseat. "Shouldn't we recite him his rights?"

"Yep. Knock yourself out. It's a full ten minutes down to the jail. It'll be good practice."

Once they were loaded up in the front seat, Green turned around to perform his due diligence, but Boris was already passed out again, leaning to the side as much as he could with the seatbelt around him.

"So, um." Green looked from Boris to Valance for a signal of where to go from there.

The FTO waved him off. "We can do it once we get to jail."

"No one will care?"

Valance chuckled. "No. No one will care."

"Okay. It just seems like he deserves to know—"

"He knows his rights just fine," Valance said curtly. "A goddamn scrubbing and some solid medical attention, that's what he deserves. And it's what Becky Hellstrom deserves to provide for his crap-coated body."

"Who?"

Valance glanced over. "One of the jail nurses. When you meet her, you'll understand. If you come right out and tell her she's an old shriveled taint, she'll make your life hell. But you can bring her all the transients your heart desires, and it's her job to care for them, sometimes wash them, and she can't do a single thing to stop you."

When Green wasn't sure what to say, Valance added, "You'll see. Trust me. Get to know her a little bit and you'll have to resist the urge to paint eyes and a mouth on a potato sack of shit to drop off for her at intake."

"That bad?" Green asked.

Valance's eyes narrowed on the road ahead. "Worse. Just wait. You'll be wishing Boris's dingleberries were dingle-grapefruits, just so she has to suffer through them. Swear to God."

Speaking of Boris, his smell started to fill the car, and when Green coughed against it, Valance grinned. "Try having a nose like mine," she said. "But if I can get over it, a human like you can, too. You'll learn to ignore it."

"Right," Green said slowly, "because you're a …" He let the sentence hang, hoping Valance would finish it for him.

Which she did. "Werewolf. Shit, Green, you really can't tell?"

Green remained silent, feeling his face heat up.

Valance sighed. "Let's hope you develop a knack for it, then. Or else—and don't take this the wrong way—you're fuuucked."

CHAPTER TWO

The jail seemed busy for four a.m., but then again, Green had little to compare it to. It was his first visit, but clearly no one cared about that fun fact. None of the other officers seemed to have a speck of energy to spare for caring about anything outside of getting out of there as soon as possible.

Green had been to *a* jail once, but it was back in his hometown of Bowers, which meant the cells and benches were almost entirely occupied with humans, one of whom had been his no-good cousin Harris, whose bail had been the reason for the visit. That had been just after bar close, and one of the men at intake had noted that it was what they called "rush hour."

But Kilhaven didn't have a set bar close—those things stayed open all night, which often meant the bars offered side rooms to sleep it off. While that seemed like an unhealthy level of enabling for alcoholics, he understood why the city had voted for it as a last-ditch effort to keep those idiots off the road.

Officer Valance pushed a slightly sobered Boris ahead of

her, using the man as a makeshift battering ram to cut through the crowd of drowsy drunks, many of whom leaned up against whatever sturdy object they could find while in various forms of shifted state—some vastly more monstrous to look at than others.

Green tried not to stare. He was a human in a diverse city of creatures. He needed to pull it together and show some cultural sensitivity, not gawk at the—

Oh God almighty! Is that …?

Valance caught a glimpse of it, too, and scrunched up her nose as her eyes searched for the closest officer to the slumped over man on the bench. "Grey! That your guy?"

Officer Grey broke off a conversation with another cop and looked at Valance, his eyes going wide in a fight-or-flight response before he composed himself. "Huh?"

Valance nodded at the suspect again. "That your guy?"

"Yeah. What's up?"

Valance handed off Boris's handcuffed wrists to Green then pulled off her gloves, shoving them in her pants pocket. "*What's up?* Look at the man's shorts! Fly's down, and his reptilian cock's out. Nobody needs to see that shit."

Valance grimaced and turned back to Green, but didn't take hold of Boris again. "What a fuck-up." She nodded forward and Green took the hint, trying not to shove Boris into too many people in the crowded room ahead of them.

"Was that suspect a—"

Valance nodded curtly. "Were-turtle by the looks of it. I bet the academy didn't teach you how to identify were-beasts by their exposed, flaccid cocks, did they?"

Green shook his head.

"Well, get used to being an expert in things you wish you didn't know."

The transient stumbled in Green's arms but easily regained his balance, crying, "Brutality!"

"Does it make you feel good to say that?" Valance grumbled. "If it makes you feel good, then by all means, shut the fuck up."

As they reached the intake desk, Green could sense every set of eyes on him as he stood next to Valance, who seemed to clear out a small bubble of space around her wherever she went.

Yet the focus was on him. The other officers and suspects could tell he was human, no doubt about it. He was impressed that anyone could pick up his scent among the smorgasbord of excrement wafting around this place.

"Dammit, woman! Out of my mind!" Valance barked at the person sitting behind the desk. Green leaned to the side to peer around Boris, curious about who was on the receiving end of Valance's wrath.

The young woman wore a sweet smile on her round, innocent face, despite Valance's harsh words to her. Brown hair framed her jaw in a short bob, and she was easily the prettiest and least loathsome thing Green had laid eyes on all night. Then he saw her name tag.

Nurse Hellstrom.

This? *This* was the taint Valance had warned him about? She didn't look like a taint. Granted, Green hadn't seen all that many taints in his life—and he assumed Valance meant it figuratively, though the connotations of the word weren't entirely clear to him.

Nurse Hellstrom turned her attention to Green. "A human. Okay then. It's nice to speak aloud."

"Huh?"

"She's a telepath," Valance said, her eyes remaining

glued to the nurse. "I forget they don't work on your kind. Shit. Almost makes me want to be human. And that's saying something."

Valance's vitriol didn't affect the warmth that emanated from Hellstrom, though. Maybe Valance just didn't like nice people. The aversion would fit with her aesthetic, at least.

"It's actually a huge relief to not get glimpses of your thoughts," Nurse Hellstrom said, her cheeks growing rosy as her smile widened. "Sometimes I accidentally hear more than I'd like to."

"Nuh-uh." Valance shook her head at Green. "Don't let her sell you that horseshit. Ain't nothing accidental about what she does. Let me"—she shut her eyes tight, a crease forming above her nose, and slammed a flat palm on the desk as she opened them—"Holy hell! Stop poking around! I can feel when you're in there!" She nodded at Boris but addressed Green. "You can take him back with that succubus. I'm gonna to get some coffee and see what I can't shake loose from the vending machine. I'm sure the nurse will be happy to show you the ropes."

When Green nodded, Valance stormed off.

"Looks like you won the FTO lottery," Hellstrom said, pulling Green's attention back to her. When she bit back a grin, Green realized it was a joke. She was being sarcastic.

Ah. I should laugh. So, he did, and immediately she stood from her chair, revealing a plump hourglass figure that had been hidden behind the desk. She motioned for Green to follow her through a set of double doors then down a hallway with rooms opening on either side.

Boris spoke out of the corner of his mouth. "She's kinda hot, ain't she? Bet you're glad I gave you an excuse to come down here and check her out."

Green ignored him and followed the nurse into an examination room.

"Have him sit on the bed," she instructed as she went over to a small table and slipped on gloves. She returned with a blood pressure monitor in hand. "Can you lift up his sleeve, please?"

Green did his best, but the jacket was heavy and stiff with dirt, dried sweat, and who knew what else. Once it was just above the elbow, she stopped him. "That's fine." She slipped the Velcro band the rest of the way under and pumped in the air.

"Mr. Romanov, did you take any drugs this evening?"

He nodded. "A few."

"Will you tell me?"

An uneven grin turned his cracked lips. "I'd rather you went looking for it."

She cocked her head slightly to the side, and her nostrils flared almost imperceptibly. "Very well." She checked the blood pressure reading and wrote it down on a chart, then checked the box next to "telepathic search (w/ permission)."

Green waited as the silent exchange proceeded in front of him, with Hellstrom narrowing her eyes intently at Boris, who moaned lecherously.

Nurse Hellstrom broke the silence. "You're lucky to be alive, Mr. Romanov."

Boris scoffed. "Dunno if lucky's the term."

"What was it?" Green asked.

The nurse sighed. "Mouthwash, grass, chalk, and feed."

"Oh wow," Green said. Then he made a quick mental note to look up what those were all street terms for, and then triple underlined said mental note. Well, mouthwash,

21

he knew. Grass he *thought* he knew, but he was starting to doubt even that. Chalk and feed? Sheesh, could be anything. Antifreeze and rat poison? Or maybe the two mixed? If the academy taught him anything, it was that everything he thought he knew about chemistry and what could take down a living being was wrong.

Once she established that Boris probably wouldn't die tonight, Green helped him to stand. With one last nod to Nurse Hellstrom, he headed back out into the intake area to find Officer Valance.

But Valance was nowhere to be seen, and Green felt panic swell up inside him as he wondered what to do next. Should he drag Boris around jail looking for the FTO, or should he just wait where he was?

"You take me to get fingerprinted next," Boris offered helpfully.

"Oh hush," Green said, then immediately began doubting whether that was the right response. The way it'd come out sounded more like Boris had just flirted with him in a bar, and he'd coyly brushed off the advance. But surely "shut your fucking hobo mouth" wouldn't go over well with the other officers in earshot. Okay, maybe there was an in between to be found.

But before he could decide on it, Valance came strolling out of a side room down the hall, an open bag of potato chips in hand. She popped a big one in her mouth and crunched down before addressing Boris. "You gonna live, B-Rat?"

"Yeah, man!"

Valance sighed. "That's a shame." She glanced at Green. "You learning things?"

Green nodded.

"Fantastic. Got plenty more lessons to learn tonight. Let's finish getting him processed. You mind being the one that touches him for a while?" She lifted the bag of chips demonstratively then added, "I just washed my hands."

Green pushed Boris ahead of him, wondering just how many more of Valance's lessons his brain could handle in a single night.

CHAPTER THREE_

The first faint glow of daylight broke the horizon, causing the city smog to radiate a muddy orange. Green sat in the driver's seat, exhaustion settling into his bones.

Day one of field training was almost at an end. One down, thirty-one more to go. And then Green was on his own.

Valance jabbed at the screen attached to the dashboard. "These fucking HAMs are nothing but trouble."

Man, he was starving. "Ham?"

She smacked the screen, and then it clicked what she was talking about. The Human-Accessible Monitors. Apparently, they were a fairly new addition to all the Kilhaven PD squad cars, installed right around the time humans won the right to serve in law enforcement. Even as he pursued the career himself, spending grueling months in the academy until he finally graduated in the middle of the pack, it struck him as a strange right for anyone to fight for. And the more he learned about the dirty work of policing, the stranger it seemed.

"I can mess with that if you want," Green offei taught us how to use the system in the academy."

"Course they did. Wasting time teaching everyc .ow to use the human tools rather than teaching humans how to be more like paranormals." But she leaned back and let Green work the HAM anyway.

Valance rested her head against her headrest and shut her eyes. When a call text popped up on the screen, Green wondered if he should assign to it.

"Nuh-uh," said Valance. Green looked over at her. Her eyes remained shut. Oh, right. She didn't need to see the screen to know about the call text. Man, what Green wouldn't give for telepathic abilities of any kind, even if it was just the ability to receive messages from the dispatchers. But that wasn't how he was made. He was born as the most physically inadequate creature possible, and those were just the cards he was dealt.

He'd spent his teen years loathing that fact. At least prior to adolescence, there'd been a hope that he'd emerge from the throes of puberty as something other than human. There was a slight chance that some recessive gene or genetic abnormality or whatever it was that caused a new species to reveal itself would make a grand entrance sometime in late middle school or early high school. Maybe he was just a late bloomer. But nope. Nothing. Just a plain old human like his whole family. Kiss your friends goodbye, Norman! They're all getting fangs or feathers or scales or spreading rumors about you telepathically so you can't even defend yourself, and you're stuck being the same as you ever were.

It was hard not to be bitter sometimes, even after he'd promised himself that he would overcome the adversity and make a difference despite his handicap. And he wasn't going to make a difference just sitting in this car with Valance at five a.m. while an officer was needed only a few blocks away.

"What do you mean, *nuh-uh*?" Green said. He tried to make it sound like a challenge, but he wasn't even close. *I need to work on that.*

Valance cracked one eye open and rolled her head slightly in Green's direction. "I mean, no. We're not going to that bullshit call with an hour left in our shift. An intox person calling to report a car theft that happened three hours ago? Doesn't get more bullshit than that."

"What do you mean? Intoxicated victims are the easiest targets, right?"

"Oh sure, but why did the vic take so long to report it after she discovered the car missing?"

Green tried to think, but his skills of deduction after such a long night left something to be desired. "She fell asleep? She got distracted?"

"I'd bank on the distraction option. Meaning she was distracted either ditching the car somewhere or hollering at some drug addict friend who borrowed it with permission and didn't give it back." She shook her head. "No, there's a convoluted story in there that would require wading through at least three hours of bullshit before it started to breach the surface.

"Now normally I would say let's get on it because you're on probation and don't get paid shit. The unspoken rule is to stick you on these dumbfuck calls, so you earn just enough overtime pay to eat until they pay you a respectable, legal amount. But I have hiking plans with Corporal Knox in a couple of hours. Today, we're heading back to the sub, I'm submitting your daily eval, then I'm going home."

"And you're sure Corporal Knox won't head over there instead of us?"

Valance chuckled. "Positive. She's a bit of a push-over, but don't let that fool you into thinking she's stupid. She knows better than to take a stolen vehicle report at five a.m."

Green leaned back in his seat, uneasy.

"Nope!" Valance swatted at the air around her head. "I said no, Stephanie! I'm busy teaching the rookie! Tell Harmon to get his lazy ass out there. Jesus!" She growled then muttered, "Fucking telepaths."

"So, we just sit here for an hour?" Green asked.

"Yep. Isn't that magical? But don't get used to it. And if you have any reports to catch up on, this would be the time to do them."

"Oh. Okay." Green swiveled the screen closer to him and pulled up the forms list. He scrolled through the ones from the night. He'd finished the last one, Boris's, in jail before they'd left, and it looked like all the rest were about as good as he could get them, too.

Once they got back to the substation, he'd upload them all. He still couldn't believe how slow the internet was in Kilhaven. For some reason, he'd assumed the internet in a big city would be better than what he'd had back home in Bowers. Except almost no one used it here outside of the HAMs. Humans made up only a small fraction of the population in Kilhaven, unlike Bowers, a city so human dense and creaturist any paranormal would be a fool to stick around longer than necessary.

"How about that Hellstrom?" Valance asked. "Awful creature, isn't she?"

"Uh ... maybe. I don't know. She was nice to me."

27

Valance waved that off, her eyes still shut. "Well, sure. Of course she was. She wants to hit it and quit it."

"Really?" Green hadn't meant to sound hopeful. And clearly, Valance noticed the tone, too, because she opened both eyes and turned in her seat to stare directly at him.

"Don't do it. Don't even think about it. I'm telling you not as your FTO, but as a fellow living being who doesn't want to see her devour another soul with that Venus fly trap between her legs."

"Another? You mean she does that a lot?"

"She's done it enough."

"Oh. Wait." It hadn't occurred to him to ask, but suddenly a lot of the pieces of Valance's personality and hatred for Nurse Hellstrom seemed to form a cohesive narrative. "Did she do that to you?"

Valance looked like she was about to respond, and then shut her mouth, closed her eyes, and leaned back in her seat again. "No. I've never had the gross misfortune to find any part of myself between her legs. Just trust me on this, Rookie. I'm here to teach you the lifesaving tricks the academy can't legally teach you. One of those is that, while Hellstrom may look like a ripe little pear on the outside, she's all shriveled taint on the inside."

While Green didn't quite follow along with the metaphor, he thought he understood the sentiment all the same.

Valance wasn't done yet. "You're going to see much worse things than a shit-caked transient shifter on this job, things that will scar you for life. That's a guarantee. But if you listen to any warning I give you, listen to this: Stay away from Becky Hellstrom. She is the devil."

Could this just be typical female pettiness because Nurse

Hellstrom was feminine and pretty? That didn't seem like Officer Valance's thing, but as little as he knew about paranormals, he knew even less about women. Or had Hellstrom broken Valance's heart at some point? It was possible, and as little as he knew about women, he knew even less about lesbians. So, he decided to drop it.

"I hear you," Green said.

"Good. I'm relieved to know—God dammit, Stephanie! What part aren't you getting? If I'm not going to a stolen vehicle call, I'm *definitely* not going to *that* clusterfuck."

Another call from dispatch. Green looked at the monitor. Undocumented shifter, suspected under the influence.

Valance grunted and sat up straight in her seat. "Fun fact. Last time I went to an intox shifter call, where the suspect wasn't passed out on his back like ol' Boris, the thing bit me on the ankle, and I had to get all kinds of shots. Even drunk, opossums are no joke."

"Shouldn't I learn how to handle something like that?"

"Oh sure," Valance said, looking over at Green with something close to fondness. Or maybe pity. "But you don't have to worry about seeking those out. This sector has the highest density of shifters in all of Kilhaven, and those folks love a good shot of Everclear. Or heroin. No, *especially* the heroin. The point is that you'll have plenty of opportunities to learn how to handle yourself in that scenario—if there even *is* a proper way to do it—but we don't have to deal with that tonight."

She nodded ahead of the car. "Let's get outta here."

Green drove to the exit of the lot, and when he put on his right blinker, Valance said, "God dammit, Green. You're already making me regret letting you drive. You turn left here, not right."

"But the substation is—"

"Only fifteen minutes away if you turn right. You think Sergeant Montoya is going to be thrilled with us showing up a little over a half-hour before the end of a shift?"

"Oh. Probably not."

"Sure as shit not. Listen up. You'll want to pay attention to this route. It's the longest possible one you can take from the jail to the substation without drawing attention to yourself. And it starts by going left." He pulled out of the lot and onto the street, taking a left where any sane person with a sense of direction would have taken a right.

"Sometimes I wonder why they even bother sending you through the academy," Valance griped, "with everything they forget to teach you."

Green was starting to wonder the same thing.

CHAPTER FOUR

Valance, at least, must have had a refreshing and restful weekend, including a nice hike with Corporal Knox. When a call came through from dispatch on their first shift of the week, as Valance and Green sat in the car after a meritless noise disturbance call, the FTO shut her eyes and said, "I'm on it, Stephanie. Of course! Oh, come on, Steph, you know I never meant that … No, no. Those cookies were amazing. Ha! Oh, hush. Of course. Yep. Nope. Green and I are all over it."

As Valance carried on with the dispatcher, Green turned his attention to the monitor for the human-impaired and read off the call. *Body found. Crossbow injuries. Victim appears to be were-bear.*

Geesh. This didn't sound pretty. Although, even on week two of field training, Green knew that "pretty" wasn't part of the job description. Neither were "friendly," "clean," or "sweet-smelling."

"Hostile," "shit-smeared," and "putrescent," on the other hand …

They ran lights and sirens all the way to the scene, Green trying to hide the thrill of driving so dangerously and with such impunity. Valance almost seemed giddy, though she contained it well as she radioed to their shift mates along the way.

"Fang 9-01 to 9-02. You think the vic might be Ursa?" Valance said into her handheld.

A crackly female's voice responded with, "Fang 9-02 to 9-01. Seems likely, judging by location and caller's description."

Valance set down the radio. "Hot damn. And it's not even my birthday."

It was a neighborhood like any other in Fang sector, meaning nothing outside of working this job could've convinced Green to set foot in it. Each house was more of a hovel, some lacking proper roofs, others with roofs that seemed to be held up only by a few wooden two-by-fours propped under the eaves.

When they arrived on scene, two cars already bathed the lot in blue and red. Officer Aliyah Brooks and Officer Patrick Harmon stood on the side of a car that blocked access to the driveway.

Green hadn't yet gotten a firm read on Brooks. She seemed friendly enough, tough in a feisty southern kind of way. She might say "bless your heart" while standing over your unconscious body that she was responsible for making unconscious. She was lithe, had warm hazel eyes and brown skin a few shades darker than Green's, and he had zero clue if she were human or paranormal. He suspected paranormal, based on her confidence, but he'd be damned if he just came out and asked. It seemed rude and/or dangerous.

Harmon was someone Green had liked immediately.

Older by perhaps fifteen or twenty years, soft spoken except when it came to his fervent religious beliefs, Harmon reminded Green of his youth pastor back home in Bowers, except he was pretty sure Harmon could pass a background check, considering he was a cop.

As Valance and Green rounded the hood, the body came into view, lying by Brooks's and Harmon's feet.

"Oh, Christ." Green tried not to let the shock of it knock him back a step. Showing fear would do him no good. And Valance seemed to think it was no big deal. "Is he dead?" Green asked before realizing it was a dumb question.

"No," Brooks said. "This poor sucker's just half-shifted and napping in someone else's driveway with an arrow through his skull."

The victim lay flat on his back, and the arrow's shaft and fletching jutted out from the hole just next to the bridge of his nose. The impact was far from a clean one, and much of the skull was caved in. Green found himself wishing his first dead body could have been the result of natural causes, maybe someone died in their sleep with a smile on their face. Ease himself in a bit.

But nope. He got a punctured were-bear with the body of a human and the arms and legs of a bear. What a nightmare.

Valance squatted down to examine the victim's face. "Yep. This is Ursa alright. You can still see a little bit of the tattoo." She pointed toward the vic's forehead then stood. "I'm almost tempted to thank him for getting that 'cop killer' tattoo to help us identify his corpse, but he's a piece of shit. And he's dead, so."

Harmon nodded toward Green. "This your first dead body, Rookie?"

Green swallowed and nodded slightly.

Harmon walked around to stand next to Green, also staring down at the body. He placed a firm hand on Green's shoulder. "So," he continued, "did you expect it to be this … grizzly?"

Brooks bit back a grin and ran a hand over her mouth to keep from laughing.

It took a moment before Green got it. Then his eyes widened.

Valance wasn't laughing, though, and Green found it oddly comforting that someone else in this small group still found death to be a serious—

"First dead body is a heavy burden … to bear," Valance said.

Brooks couldn't hold it in this time, and she cackled. Even Officer Valance let herself chuckle, and when she did, Green noticed for the first time that the woman might be pretty if she weren't so goddamn scary.

"I'm fine," Green replied, trying to sound like a good sport, hoping they couldn't hear the waver in his voice.

"Great," said Valance. "Then why don't you take the lead on this?"

"Hmm?" Green felt his shoulders turn into knots.

"The lead. You got this, right?" The corner of her lip twitched. "I mean, it's not like you'll fuck up and he'll get deader because of it."

Green cleared his throat. "Yeah. No. I mean, I got it. Yeah, I'll take the lead."

He turned to Officer Patrick Harmon, a fifteen-year veteran who'd stayed on patrol rather than advancing through the ranks for the sole reason of being a complete lazy ass. The older man stared at him bemusedly, but not with any obvious hostility. "Tell me where you want me."

Green inhaled deeply and tried not to start with "uh," or "um." He thought back to the steps he'd learned in the academy. "Call out homicide detectives." He turned to Brooks. "Tape off the scene. I'll set down some evidence markers." He turned to Valance and almost missed the split second of surprise in her eyes before she narrowed them at him and his words tripped in his throat. "Um. Grab the camera for some shots. And the evidence markers."

"You sure?" she asked.

He'd been less sure of very few things in his life. "Uh, yes?" She shrugged and went to grab the camera. "I'll stand watch until you get back."

"Fucking genius idea, Rookie. We don't want him going anywhere when our backs are turned."

As much as he knew she was trying to make him feel like an idiot, he also knew he was following protocol, no matter how much she'd succeeded in her mission.

When she returned, she moved to stand next to Green where he stared down at the body. He couldn't take his eyes off of it. He knew a dead were-bear shouldn't freak him out like this because he was a cop now. But why the fuck *wouldn't* a murdered were-bear freak him out? That seemed like the natural response. But no one else appeared to be experiencing that.

Once Brooks and Harmon finished their assigned tasks, they rejoined Green by the body. "I wasn't sure if he was dead at first," Brooks said from behind him. "I had to *paws* and take a closer look."

Harmon chuckled from the other side of the victim's body, and damn the sound was welcoming and friendly, which only left Green more conflicted about his fellow officer. On the one hand, Harmon was someone to be

35

respected, yet another imposing figure on the toughest shift in Kilhaven. But on the other hand, if Harmon laughed at inappropriate things, it wrecked Green's view of him as a paternalistic presence and lessened the possibility that Green would eventually slip and call him Dad.

Harmon looked up at Green. "I pulled a gun off the body before you got here, but then I put it back."

Green inhaled so quickly he choked on his spit. "You what? Why would you do that?" Oh, God. Evidence tampering while he was the lead officer on the call? Was there a supplemental report he'd have to fill out for that?

Harmon remained calm. "He has a right to *bear arms*."

There was nothing about this that didn't feel wrong.

Kilhaven Police didn't exactly have the best relationship with the Kilhaven community, and if the media caught wind of this, it wouldn't make the tenuous relationship any stronger, Green was sure of that. Luckily, he didn't see any elves hanging around, and the officers had the sense to say it off air.

But Brooks cackled at the joke. "So much for you being the religious one."

Harmon shrugged and adjusted his belt. "My God happens to have a great sense of humor about death, thank you very much."

Brooks shrugged. "I won't argue there. Green, you need anything else from me?"

A loud gurgling noise made Green jump, and he looked down at the body in front of him where the noise originated. Then came a smell. It was like *eau d'Boris*, only more pungent, fresher. An image of the Grim Reaper farting —really ripping a solid one, aiming it right at the dead were-bear on the ground—popped into Green's head, and that was about the last visual he needed to add to his already disturbing night.

When he saw a flash of light on the body, he turned to see Valance standing behind him with her digital camera. "Not exactly a *Kodiak* moment, huh?" She chuckled to herself, and Harmon nodded his approval.

Valance handed Green the markers, and he began setting them down where personal items had fallen out of the pockets of the victim—a pen cap, half a used joint, a credit card. He glanced across the body at Valance and she crouched down to snap a close-up of the arrow's entry point.

Brooks stepped out of the way so Valance could move around, then frowned. "Don't you think this is more a job for a *polar*oid camera?"

Valance didn't look up, but offered a bent elbow her way, and Brooks bumped it with her own elbow.

Green couldn't take anymore. With each lame pun, his paranoia mounted. "I love the humor, don't get me wrong," he lied, "but what happens if someone overhears?"

Harmon glanced at Green only for a moment before tossing a bemused frown at Valance. She returned the look, shrugged slightly, and then stood, turning to her officer in training.

"Trust me. We are fully aware of the situation. And in all seriousness, this vic is not really a vic. He has multiple felony arrests for paranormal trafficking. If anything, someone shooting him in the face with a crossbow has saved the department a whole headache, since it was only a matter of time before one of our officers ended up putting a silver bullet through his muzzle." Her eyes flickered down to Green's slightly open mouth, and she sighed, tucked the camera into her vest, and rested her hands on her duty belt.

"I get it. You're new. You've never seen a dead body. You still think death is some meaningful event we're supposed to learn from. We've all been there." She patted him on the shoulder, and her blue eyes seemed to soften. "It takes about a year before you can, you know, get your *bear*ings." She winked at him, smacked him on the bicep, and then went back to snapping pictures.

———

The were-bear incident had eaten up most of the night, and as Green and Valance headed back to the substation after catching up the homicide detectives, Green realized he was actually impressed by how many bear puns everyone had managed over the past five hours. The detectives were the most skilled in the wordplay, with Detective Burns managing to sneak in a deadpan "cubbie" pun over the radio that even the shrewdest of reporters would have a hard time proving was intentional. But then again, the detectives had more experience on the job, and there was a reason they were paid the big bucks, Green supposed.

But it still didn't sit right with him. A few things had become seared into Green's eyelids while standing watch over Henry Franco Morrison—or as the rest of his shift knew him, Ursa—like the texture and subtle shades of brown in the man's fur on his right front paw as it reflected the red and blue lights. Or the bone shard of the vic's fractured skull that had been forced out through the skin an inch below his eye and a couple inches away from the actual puncture wound. The longer Green had stared at that, the more it reminded him of a lightning bolt, especially as the camera flash glinted off of it from different angles.

"When I was active duty," Valance began, breaking the long silence, "there was this POW I was in charge of feeding and generally keeping alive."

Green tried not to gasp audibly or swerve into the shoulder at the horrifying prospect of having Valance as a sole caregiver.

"His name was Raoul or something," she continued. "Maybe Romero? Fuck it. He's dead now anyway. It doesn't matter what his name was."

Green was starting to wonder what *did* matter to Officer Valance.

"The point is that he was a were-jaguar, and those fuckers have a hair-trigger, like their brain might be a little too large to fit comfortably in their skull. Any little jostle can set them off into psycho mode. So, everyone was afraid of this guy when we captured him. Oh, and he'd killed just a ton of our troops. Like, bloodbath. Anyway, no one would touch him. But I knew something they didn't. I knew that were-jags are aggressive because they have to be. There are about fifty different pressure points on their body that hurt like hell and will render them incapacitated if you can hit one.

"Armed with that knowledge, I volunteered to watch him. Only after none of the pressure points worked to subdue him did I regret my decision terribly. Long six months short, I eventually got the better of him, and we came to an understanding, but that's a story for another time. The point is that I asked him why nothing worked on him, why none of the pressure points were tender. Was he born without nerves or something? He told me, 'La Tunda'—that's what they knew me by down there—'La Tunda—'"

"Wait, he knew your name, but you didn't bother to learn his?"

She glanced over at him, dubiously. "Uh, yeah. *Everyone* in Guatemala had heard of La Tunda."

Green decided not to ask.

Then she hurriedly added, "Oh, by the way, don't mention that to anyone. It's still not technically public knowledge that we were in Guatemala." She inhaled deeply to regain focus and then continued. "He said, 'La Tunda, I was born with more sensitive pressure points than anyone else in my village.' Well, that bullshit didn't answer my question, so I kept at him. Eventually he told me something I'll never forget. He said that some people are doomed to lives that jab at all their sensitive spots. Over time, the nerves in those areas will stop hurting as much, but in the meantime, the pain is a distraction that could cost you your life.

"This fucker had taken things into his own hands and intentionally deadened his nerves. I mean, literally. Not talking about emotions here. He'd spent months on end jabbing and poking all his pressure points until they just stopped responding. That way, when life threw things his way that would target those sensitivities—me, in this case— he was ready for it."

"Damn, that's … impressive."

"Impressive doesn't even begin to describe it, Rookie."

"What happened to him?" Green asked.

"Shit himself to death." She shrugged. "Yeah, I dunno, I guess he got a bug, and then he just started shitting and didn't stop. Happens a lot in the jungle. Guess he forgot to desensitize his bowels." She chuckled flatly. "Point is, no one outside the Force knows a nanofuck about what it takes to do this job. They want us to be sensitive and caring and show compassion at every turn. But if we did that, if we didn't proactively deaden our nerves, no one would last until retirement in this job. You gotta make a choice, and once you do, things will be a lot easier. Because you'll either quit this God-forsaken job within the first two years, or you'll commit to it and start to actively desensitize your emotional pressure points so you can deal with a dead fucking were-bear piece of shit paranormal trafficker."

"Are those my only options?" Green asked.

Valance sighed. "The only two I've found. But then again, what the hell do I know?"

CHAPTER FIVE_

"Mind the lawn chair," Valance said, keeping her composure despite the circus taking place in front them.

"What lawn—?"

A glint of moonlight off the chair's aluminum legs caught Green's eye as the object came hurtling toward his head, and he managed to duck at the last second to avoid injury.

"Mrs. Culver," Valance spoke firmly, "I'm gonna ask you to stop throwing things at your husband. You almost hit an officer, and then we would've had to arrest you."

The woman ignored her and grabbed another lawn chair, waving it above her head, squinting through the high beams of the police cruiser that backlit Green and Valance and flooded into the front yard of her trailer and the one next door. "Carl, you goddamn fuckup! I'm done with you! I'm done! You hear me?"

Carl didn't answer her because he was an alligator.

She threw the lawn chair at him all the same, showing strength incongruous with the middle-age woman's scrawny and pallid appearance. But that only agitated Carl, and he rocked forward at her, hissing.

Officer Valance had warned Green about what she called, "muckers," but now three weeks into field training and this was the first call they'd responded to in the swampy outer reaches of Fang sector. Valance had explained the likely reason for that on their way out to the call: the sort of people who lived in the swamps were the sort of people who didn't call the cops.

Or rather, they only call the cops when things really escalated. Like when a shifter smoked too much meth, had sex with his wife's sister, and then shifted into an alligator. For example.

"Fang 9-80 to 9-01. I'm five minutes out," came Corporal Knox's voice through Green's earpiece.

"Ma'am!" Valance said more forcefully. "You need to calm down."

The woman pointed at her husband. "Shoot him if you have to, Officer! I'm done with his cheatin' ass!"

"We're not going to shoot him, ma'am," Green said hastily.

The woman turned her rabid attention on him then. "The hell you got silver bullets for, if not shooting garbage like Carl? Shit! Why did I even bother calling you out here?"

When Mrs. Culver turned and headed inside, Carl turned laboriously toward Green and Valance, who kept a solid twenty yards between them and the predator.

"What'd they teach you about gators in the academy?" Valance asked out of the corner of her mouth.

"Nothing. But I know they can't see directly ahead of them."

"Oh, wonderful." She nodded. "If this bastard charges, we just need to run in a straight line?"

"I guess—"

"Oh, for fuck's sake," Valance said, her hands hovering at the ready by her belt. "No. You don't run from the situation."

"So what, we shoot him?"

"Normally, yes, but she's a meth head, and giving meth heads what they want is called enabling, and it's wrong. Plus, we're not goddamn animal control to be called out here whenever it's time to put a shifter down—which is most of the time anyway. And believe you me, she might be asking us to shoot him right now, but as soon as we pull that trigger, she'll change her mind, and then we'll have all these muckers so stirred up, cops won't be able to set foot out here for another year at least."

The gator gurgled then growled and lunged laboriously toward the officers.

"What about Tasers?" Green asked.

Valance shook her head. "No. I mean, be my guest. But if that dickhead charges and you're close enough to tase it, kiss at least one leg goodbye. *If* you hit the thing, and *if* the prongs penetrate the skin, you'll only stun the thing for five seconds at most. Don't think a five-second head start is going to be enough against a pissed off, recently tased animal that's about as close to motherfucking dinosaurs as it gets."

"Okay, then what do we do?"

The gator's wife tore out of the house, charging straight at Carl dangling a small fluffy object high in the air in front of her. "God dammit, Carl! You no-good, inbred motherfucker!"

Valance responded immediately, despite the live, methed-out alligator, and jetted across the muddy lawn to grab the woman around the waist before she could end up within striking distance of her husband. "Ma'am! I need you to calm down."

The woman didn't appear aware that she was being physically restrained by law enforcement, as on the verge of hysterics as she was. She shook the long, fluffy thing harder at her husband. "Where is she, Carl?"

Green squinted at the object in her hand, trying to make some sense of the situation. It looked like a limp duster, except it was orange and a little fluffier than what might be useful for housework.

When was the last time I dusted anything? I should do that if I survive this.

When the gator hissed again, Mrs. Culver shouted, "Really, Carl? Dame Flufferkins?" She shook the limp object demonstratively. "You knew I liked her best, you sonofabitch! You knew I liked her!"

Officer Valance's eyes locked onto the object, and she crinkled up her nose but continued restraining the hysterical woman.

"Why the fuck did I make your lazy ass a pot roast if your dumbfuck, no-good shifter self is just gonna get high and eat my goddamn *cat*!" She whipped her head around to Green. "Well? Shoot him! Why's this taking so long?"

"Ma'am," Green responded, "we are absolutely not going to shoot your—"

The woman's arm that held the cat's tail flew backward, her elbow connecting with Valance's jaw, and Green sucked in air as he saw Mrs. Culver's life flash before his eyes.

Valance's head snapped back upon impact, but that was

about all the reaction she had. Green would've sooner stuck an arm in Carl's toothy mouth than throw an elbow to Valance's face.

Officer Valance twisted one of the woman's arms at a funny angle behind her back a millisecond before landing a hard chop to the crook where her neck met her shoulder, and the woman crumpled.

Valance went for her cuffs and clicked them on the woman in a movement so smooth and practiced it reminded Green of one of the human magicians from his hometown performing a flawless illusion.

"Fuck you, you creature-hatin' murderer!" Mrs. Culver shouted.

If it hurt Valance's feelings to be called that, she didn't let on, unless throwing the woman facedown into the muddy yard and driving a knee into the small of her back was the way Valance showed emotions, which, upon consideration, Green thought likely.

"Jenny!" Mrs. Culver shouted.

Jenny? Who the hell is Jenny?

Green followed the woman's sightline and saw that a neighbor had finally peeked her head out of a nearby trailer.

"Jenny, you see this brutality? You see it?" Mrs. Culver hollered.

Something large lurched forward ahead of Green and dragged his attention away from the melodrama. Oh right. The tweaker gator.

"I can't breathe! You're putting too much pressure on me!" Carl's wife shouted from the ground.

"Unless your lungs and ovaries swapped places at some point, you're fine," Valance spat back.

The woman's moaning and hollering must've riled up

Carl, who hissed and took off straight for Green. With no actual plan for how to address this situation, Green pulled his Taser free and, deciding his left foot was probably the least important of the two, braced with that foot slightly forward as a sacrifice to the ancient reptilian gods.

Twenty-five feet. That was the max range of the Taser. And when the target was at max range, it meant the two prongs, both of which not only had to make contact with but *stick* into the suspect's skin, were at their maximum distance apart from one another. If they hit, that meant a bigger circuit of muscles contracting, but from everything he'd learned in the academy, it was unusual for both to make contact from that range successfully. And at such a low angle, Green felt sure they would glance off the gator's thick skin, and he would be toast. He would have to wait until Carl was much, much closer than twenty-five feet.

But as the gator closed the distance quickly, something inside Officer Green's head said, "Nuh-uh" and he stuck the Taser back into place on his belt and drew his gun instead. Survival instinct, that's what it was.

And then it dawned on him as Carl hesitated in his charge, that the gator didn't seem to know where Green had gone since he was standing right where the gator's eyes couldn't see.

That was little consolation when the massive jaws hung open only three feet away from where Green stood stock still with his gun drawn.

"Shoot him!" Mrs. Culver shouted.

The noise drew her husband's attention, and at that moment Green knew two things: first, now that the gator had turned his head, Green's temporary hiding spot was toast; second, this was his chance.

He shoved his gun back into his holster and leaped forward.

It had never been on Green's bucket list to wrestle an alligator, but here he was, clinging to the ten-foot-long beast's back with all his might, doing little to secure the scene other than proving a serious distraction to Carl, who wriggled and writhed to shake Green loose.

Green held on for dear life, because if he were knocked loose, it'd for sure be over. He hooked his hands together beneath the gator neck and rode the meth head like a bronco. And even amid the chaos, a part of his brain was acutely aware that he looked like a fucking idiot.

A new set of police lights flooded the scene, but Green had no time for that.

He remembered one tidbit about alligators a second before it became lethal, but not soon enough to prevent it from happening.

Alligators barrel roll. If the weight of Carl rolling over onto him didn't crush all his ribs, it would at least cause him to lose his grip.

When Carl rolled, Green tensed his body, shut his eyes, and braced for the pain.

But the gator had hardly exposed its belly when Green heard a loud pop and Carl convulsed, squirming free of Green's grasp and flying five feet in the air. By the time he hit the ground again, he was a fully naked human.

Green leaped on him, pinning him to the ground and hoping the man was too stunned to shift right away.

Someone shoved him gently to the side, and he looked up to see Corporal Knox bending down. She clicked the silvers on him, pinning him face down in the mud with his hands behind him, placing her knee on his lower back the same way Valance was doing with his wife.

When Carl resorted to his last available defense mechanism, farting loudly and unabashedly, Knox crinkled her nose.

"I swear these swamps are more methane than oxygen," she said, panting against the adrenaline. "Green, go secure the Taser."

He did as he was told, and the jumble of events over the past ten seconds began to fall into line as he found her shifter-specific Taser feet away from where Carl was pinned to the ground, the cartridge still attached, the wires leading in a trail that ended somewhere underneath Carl's body.

Knox must've sunk the prongs of her high-powered Taser into Carl's belly when he rolled. Green picked it up off the ground and turned it over in his hand. Damn, it would be nice if each officer could carry one of these, but as it was, the department didn't want to shell out for it, so only the corporals and sergeants were provided with one.

Corporal Knox surveyed the scene, and her eyes slowly opened wide as she looked from Valance to the yelling woman beneath her. "What happened here?"

"Brutality!" Mrs. Culver screamed.

Valance ignored her. "She assaulted me." She pointed at the naked man with long, scraggly hair beneath Knox. "And he ate the cat."

"Bullshit!" Carl's wife shouted. "I didn't assault your lying ass." She craned her neck to look across the yard at Corporal Knox. "He did eat Dame Flufferkins, though. That part's true."

"Whatever," Knox said. "Let's get them in the cars, and we'll sort this out." She pulled Carl to his feet, and it was a bit of a pleasant surprise that the naked man's front was so caked in mud that Green didn't have to get an eyeful.

As she passed him, Knox said, "Nice work there, Officer. Didn't know you had it in you to wrestle a gator. Not the most effective, but it worked as long as it had to, to keep everyone safe. Just don't forget to fill out the response to resistance paperwork before you go home."

She hollered back over her shoulder at Valance, who yanked Mrs. Culver to her feet with more force than necessary, "Put that in his daily eval, Valance. I know you'll forget to give him credit for it at the final eval, and even *you* gotta admit that was ballsy."

"Yeah, yeah," Valance said apathetically. "I guess it wasn't the dumbest thing he's done."

Husband and wife were situated in separate backseats. They kept Carl in his silvers but put his wife, IDed as Greta Culver—human and longtime pain in the ass of law abiding citizens who apparently weren't thrilled with their car being stolen—in the low-urgency iron cuffs.

Green noticed Valance slowly working out her jaw as he approached her where she stood in front of their shared car. A silver-dollar-size bump had already risen from the space just below her right eye.

"You need some ice or something?" Green asked.

"Oh sure. You got some?" she asked without bothering to look at him.

Immediately he realized how dumb of a question it was. "Uh, no."

She grinned. "Then you're just being a cock tease. You get the neighbor's statement already?"

Green sighed. "Yeah, she said, uh, that she saw you hit

Mrs. Culver and then throw her to the ground and continue to hit her long after she was unconscious."

Valance sighed. "I wish. Okay, and you told her that lying on an official report is against the law?"

Green nodded.

"Great. That'll do. Let's get these two lovebirds to jail." She sniffed and then winced. "Goddamn. If only we were allowed to change on duty. She wouldn't've gotten a cheap shot in if I'd been able to wolf out on her right away."

"Couldn't you just have requested special permission from Sergeant Montoya?"

"Well of course, but that takes time. Plus, that man's more politician than police; he never approves those requests. Maybe someday the city council will get its head out of its ass and leave it up to each officer's discretion when we can change on duty." She chuckled. "Nah, that'll never happen. Far be it from our brave elected-officials-slash-former-high-school-class-presidents to allow us to use all our resources to do this impossible and futile job."

Green nodded and silently hoped to whatever deity might be listening that he never witnessed what kind of carnage would inevitably follow Valance changing into a wolf.

CHAPTER SIX_

Green wondered if he'd ever get used to the smell of jail. It was like a war of attrition between sour excrement and industrial-strength bleach.

Valance insisted that a cold drink from the vending machine was the only thing that would make her face any better, though the logic of that eluded Green entirely. She split from him and Carl as soon as they were through the double-door security of the jailhouse and had gotten Carl set up with some prison clothes to cover his post-shift nakedness. That was fine, though. Green could easily manage Carl on his own, as long as the silvers stayed on him. The meth head had become somewhat more subdued on the long ride to jail anyway.

The night had been such a whirlwind from the moment Green and Valance had arrived in the swampy trailer park that he'd almost forgotten who he might encounter at intake.

Nurse Hellstrom was busy typing a report when he

arrived, but as soon as he cleared his throat, she swiveled in her chair and beamed up at him. "Officer Green! Good to see you again."

She remembers my name.

Then he remembered that it was written on his chest, so there was that. Had her eyes flickered down to his lapel, though? He didn't think so.

After providing the information for the perp, Nurse Hellstrom led Green and Carl down the hall to the examination room, where she went through what Green was starting to glean as a standard set of questions: creature type, known medical conditions, drugs taken recently.

For the creature type, Carl grunted, "Shifter, you dumb bitch."

For known medical conditions, Carl grunted, "Dumbfuck wife and a silver allergy, you dumb bitch."

And for drugs taken recently, Carl was somewhat more straightforward but equally impolite as he said, "Ketamine, then some meth to perk me up, then some more meth because it was fun, you dumb bitch."

Green's mouth fell open each time Carl insulted Nurse Hellstrom, but the nurse didn't seem fazed in the least. Finally, after the third instance, Green shook Carl by the handcuffs. "That's no way to talk to her."

Becky's eyes flashed onto Green. She smiled, but this wasn't just a sunny smile of appreciation; this was something much less innocent. "Thank you, Officer Green, but I don't come to work each day for the warm affection. I usually seek that after hours."

Green felt a knot form in his lower abdomen. Was she ...?

She addressed Carl. "Do you give me consent for a mental search?"

He grinned, exposing his yellow teeth and the blackness around his gums. "You a telepath?"

Nurse Hellstrom nodded.

Carl's grin grew. "Fucked a telepath once." He glanced back over his shoulder at Green. "You know what the best part about fucking a telepath is?"

Green did not, in fact, know anything about sex with a telepath, and while he found himself suddenly overcome with curiosity, now didn't seem like the time. "You need to watch your mouth."

Carl went on anyway. "Best part is that she can tell when your wife's coming home from her sister's down the street."

Nurse Hellstrom rolled her eyes. "Do you consent to the search?"

Carl eyed her in a way that made Green want to smash out a few of the man's crumbling teeth. "You know what the second-best part of fucking a telepath is?"

"Nobody cares," Green said, his heart rate increasing with each new mention of sex.

"How good it feels to be inside her while she's inside you."

Nurse Hellstrom sighed. "Is that a yes?"

Carl winked at her, his eyelid staying shut so long that Green began to wonder if it wasn't actually just a stroke the man was suffering. "More like a fuck yes, you naughty nurse. Undress me with your mind."

"Dude, really?" Green said, before realizing how unprofessional of a reaction that was.

But as soon as Nurse Hellstrom was given verbal consent, she focused in on Carl's lesion-covered face, and the man went silent, his eyes rolling back into his head in ecstasy.

Green had an overwhelming impulse to leave the room and give the two some privacy.

"Oh wow, Mr. Culver, I'm impressed," the nurse said. "You were able to shift into a gator and back without the baggie falling out? I didn't know the anatomy of an alligator's anus would allow for such a thing during a shift." She stood briskly. "Either way, I'm gonna need you to stand, lean against that wall over there, and drop your pants."

Green's impulse to leave the room only grew. "He's got something up … there?"

"Sure as shit." She giggled then bit her bottom lip.

Green allowed himself a small chuckle, too, and helped Carl pull down his pants.

The baggie of crystal meth took a little coaxing, but finally, when Carl's fake coughing launched him into a bout of real coughing, the thing popped free and fell on the floor.

Hellstrom pointed at it. "You should get that for evidence."

"Oh. Right."

Green reached for it but paused when Hellstrom cleared her throat loudly. He looked up at her, and she mouthed "gloves" at him.

Elch. Yeah. Good call.

The exam room had evidence bags in the corner, probably for this exact sort of discovery, and Green made quick work of bagging it before disposing of his gloves.

Once the exam was concluded and Nurse Hellstrom was sure there was nothing else concealed in any orifice of Carl Culver's body, Green led the man back toward the intake area, hoping to find Valance without much trouble. But before he could get a step outside the room, Nurse Hellstrom said, "Oh wait, Officer Green. You forgot something." He turned slightly toward her, hoping whatever it was wasn't covered in Carl's crap, and she moved close and slipped something in his shirt pocket. "You might want that for later."

He didn't get a good look at what it was, but that didn't matter because she was touching him. Being that close to her, taking in her sweet scent—God, she was like an oasis in this desert of stank.

"Thanks," he said, then quickly turned and shoved Carl harder than he'd meant to out the door.

Valance was already waiting for him at the front desk. She tilted back a bag of chips, patting it to get the last crumbs, then crumpled it and set it on the desk in front of Nurse Hellstrom's chair. "Sorry to stick you with that succubus again." She reached forward, her eyes on Carl's cuffs. "Here. I'll take him to get fingerprinted, and you can get something from the break room. Your adrenaline's going to nosedive after that *totally unnecessary*"—she looked Carl in the eyes as she stressed the words—"gator encounter, and the only thing for it is fat and sugar and caffeine."

This was way more caring than Green expected from Valance, and he decided not to press his luck and to simply do what she'd said. Which in this case was easy since a candy bar and a soda sounded a little like heaven in this worldly wasteland.

A half-dozen officers already occupied the break room when Green entered, but the only one he recognized was Aliyah Brooks from his shift. She nodded at him and stirred a packet of sugar into the tiny Styrofoam cup of coffee in her hand. "Heard ya had a run-in with some o' those muckers."

There was that word again. Muckers. Green had never heard it before tonight, and considering he'd learned it from Officer Valance's mouth, he'd assumed it was some kind of a slur. But Brooks didn't strike him as the type to shamelessly use a creaturist slur so openly. Maybe it wasn't bad.

"Yeah, gator."

"Ya really wrestle him?" she asked amusedly.

He sighed and mumbled, "Yeah."

She chuckled and nodded at him, lifting her Styrofoam cup in a subtle salute. "Stupid and ballsy. Ya might just fit in around Fang, Rookie."

A bulky officer jumped into the conversation from his seat at the tiny fold-out table. "You should see those jokers on PCP."

A quick glance at the stripes on the man's sleeve informed Green that he was speaking with a sergeant. He nodded amicably, really putting his neck into it.

"Apparently it was ketamine and meth," Green added. "Nurse Hellstrom had to dig for the ketamine part."

Brooks sighed and rolled her eyes. "Bet she did. Stupid prying bitch."

Green paused just as he was about to slip a coin into the vending machine, his mouth lolling open slightly as he looked over at Brooks. He glanced at the sergeant to see if Brooks would be reprimanded. But the sergeant just stared down at his newspaper and sipped his coffee like nothing had been said.

"She's not that bad," Green said meekly. He wished he could have done more to stand up for the nurse, who was clearly a target of the other women in this department. But he also probably needed to stay on good terms with Brooks for the sake of staying alive on the job.

Brooks bit her bottom lip, nodding gently and staring at Green with a look of such pity that anyone who'd entered the break room at that point might've thought he'd just told her the love of his life was murdered on their wedding night. Then she shook her head slowly and said, "Nah, you're just wrong. She ain't nothing but awful."

"Well, she's been nice to me," Green groused.

Brooks chuckled again. "No shit. You're human."

Green jammed his quarters into the machine and mashed the button for a soda just a little too forcefully, sending the entire machine rocking backward. "I don't know what my species has to do with anything," he grumbled.

"It's got everything to do with it," Brooks said plainly. "Ain't encountered a lot of telepaths, huh?"

Green popped open his drink and stared at Officer Brooks. This *was* that woman thing, wasn't it? That thing where women hated other women who they thought were better looking or more feminine or intelligent. He should just drop it. The last thing he wanted to do was turn half of the Kilhaven Police Department against him by sounding sexist. "No, Brooks, I haven't encountered a lot of them." He sipped his drink so he wouldn't say anything else.

She nodded. "Then I forgive ya for being naive."

After choking just a little, he regained his composure and was about to say something when the sergeant stood up, tossed his empty Styrofoam cup in the trash, nodded at Green and said, "She's right, Rookie. Hellstrom is the devil."

Then he turned and left the break room. Brooks shrugged apologetically before following the sergeant out.

It was only then that Green remembered Nurse Hellstrom had slipped something in his pocket. He looked around, but the other officers didn't seem to care that he even existed. He reached in his shirt, felt around, and pulled out a slip of paper.

On it was the word *Becky* and a phone number.

Nurse Hellstrom wanted him.

CHAPTER SEVEN_

As soon as the late afternoon sunlight flopped lazily in between the slats of Norman Green's bedroom blinds, coating everything in a thick orange, he knew he'd made a mistake. For one, he'd overslept by about thirty minutes, which meant it was time to scramble to get ready for his shift. And that sucked because little set his hair on end more than starting a new week running behind.

There was another mistake that might not have been a mistake—he still hadn't decided for sure.

He'd considered it as best he could all morning, as his eyes had grown heavy, his dick had become completely limp, and the haze of a solid orgasm had started to lift, but still he couldn't conclude with certainty whether the events leading up to the naked woman lying next to him had been a mistake. He snuck a lecherous glance at his new companion and the shape of her naked breasts beneath his thin, white top sheet.

Becky Hellstrom was perfection.

There were pros and cons to this arrangement that

they'd both verbally agreed upon and then consummated in the early dawn hours, after her overtime shift had ended and she'd knocked on his apartment door, all curves and warm potential staring at him under thick lashes.

Pro: he got to have sex with her, and that was amazing. While his human-ness had kept him from experiencing what Carl described as a sort of circular penetration with a telepath, he was okay with that. Singular penetration was already pretty awesome, and to have her inside his mind— God help any woman who saw the montage of subconscious garbage that bubbled to the surface just before he blew his load. No, regular sex was just great. And that was the only pro to this that he could think of, but it was enough, for now at least, to balance out the cons.

Which were quite a few. First, there was the fact that he was only starting on his fourth week on the Force and already he'd broken the age-old wisdom of *don't stick your pen in the company ink*. Or, depending on how good (or bad) the sex had been for Nurse Hellstrom, perhaps also the adage of *don't shit where you eat*. It was always impossible to tell how good he was at sex, and asking a woman to give him an honest post-coital assessment had never been a thing he felt ready for in his life.

Another major con was that if anyone found out, especially Officer Valance, he would never hear the end of it. Or if people did shut up about it *eventually*, everyone would always treat him as if he were just another dumb guy who couldn't keep it in his pants.

Which, he supposed, he was.

He sat up and rolled to the edge of the mattress that he kept on the floor and reached forward, stretching, but also grabbing his boxers so that if Becky woke up, she wouldn't immediately be subjected to his morning wood. It seemed the only gentlemanly thing to do. Granted, his small-town upbringing and twenty-four years of life hadn't taught him all that much about etiquette in general, and definitely not sex etiquette, if such a thing existed. But he put on his boxers all the same.

"Where are you going?" Becky asked sleepily from her side of the bed. "Man, it's nice to ask and not already know the answer."

He glanced over his shoulder on his way to the bathroom. Damn, she looked good sleepy. Her short, brown hair was slightly matted and tousled and went well with the wild personality she'd unveiled to him a handful of hours ago when she'd shucked off her clothes and started ordering him around. "Work. I'm running late already. Valance is going to have my ass."

"You know, most people worry more about their sergeant having their ass than their FTO."

"Most people don't have Valance as an FTO. Also, I sorta have to impress her since my final review is dependent upon her daily evaluations."

He went into the attached bath and then returned with a toothbrush in his mouth.

"Do you get to see the daily evaluations?" Becky asked.

"I think so."

She sat up straighter. "You haven't asked?"

He pulled the toothbrush from his mouth, dangling it in the air. "Would you? It doesn't matter, anyway. It's hard enough to show up to work alongside Valance every day just suspecting she thinks I'm a shit cop. If I confirmed that suspicion by looking at her evaluations, I think I might never get out of bed."

She grinned at him, arching an eyebrow slightly. "That wouldn't have to be a bad thing."

Man, she's good.

"What if you're doing something wrong constantly and just don't know it because you haven't read it in the evaluations?" Becky said.

"I don't—" Talking with his mouth full was probably not sexy. He ran to the bathroom and finished brushing, then spit and rinsed before returning to dig through his closet for a clean uniform. "I don't foresee that being a problem. Valance isn't exactly shy when it comes to telling me what she thinks of my performance."

"You know, Norman, Valance isn't always this bad."

He turned to face the naked woman in his sheets. "That almost sounds like you're standing up for her." Not what he'd expected after the way Officer Valance had spoken about and treated Becky on a daily basis.

She scooted up in bed, leaning back against the wall and making Green notice for the first time that he didn't have a headboard. Didn't adults use headboards? The idea of buying one hadn't occurred to him before now.

"I'm not defending her at all. On the contrary."

He turned fully toward her and crossed his arms over his chest. "Meaning?"

"Meaning …" She paused. "I hate to be the one to say this, but she's not as mean to the rookies who aren't … human." She scrunched up her nose and frowned apologetically. "I've called her out on it a few times since obviously, I have no problem with it"—her eyes flickered to Green's exposed legs— "and of course she didn't appreciate that. I think it's why she hates me."

"Huh." That made immediate sense as things clicked

into place. Valance never did seem too happy about having humans on the Force, and it sure provided some context to why Valance hated Becky so fervently. "I guess I'll keep that in mind."

"I'm sorry, Norman. For what it's worth, I think it's bullshit that there's so much prejudice still in the Kilhaven Police. I personally love humans. You're all such puzzles, much more complex and resourceful than all of us paras. We just get lazy because each of us has a crutch of some kind."

Green reached for his balls to scratch them then caught himself before he did and braced his hand on his hip instead. "I hadn't thought about it like that."

Becky smiled. "That's probably because you're too busy managing everyone's bullshit."

"But not yours," Green said.

She chuckled airily. "No, not mine. Never mine. I don't play games, Norman. I hope you won't either."

"No games," he promised. But holy shit, was this really a conversation they were having after a single morning— albeit the rowdiest he'd ever had with a woman—and no discussion of future encounters?

Becky nodded, then her attention seemed to shift, and she nibbled her bottom lip. "Do you have to go so soon?"

"You know I do."

A furtive smile turned her lips. "I don't know that. What I do know is that I had an incredible morning with you, and my whole body is tingling just thinking about it. And I know I'm still naked under these covers." She let the top sheet, which she'd been clutching to her chest, drop to reveal her plump breasts. "And I know you have a, uh, situation that I could help you out with." Her gaze moved shamelessly downward to focus on his morning wood that could no longer be blamed entirely on having just woken up —not just because the time of day didn't happen to technically be morning, but because *oh, holy shit* a woman wanted to have sex with him a second time.

Not one to shun a miracle, Green glanced at the clock by the bed, did some quick mental math, and then, after deciding a meal before work was probably overrated, took a running leap back into bed.

CHAPTER EIGHT_

Green's empty stomach growled, loud enough this time that Valance glanced at him from the passenger's seat, raising a judgmental brow his direction. "You need me to pull over at a gas station or something?"

"Nope."

She pressed her lips together thoughtfully. "Suit yourself." Then three seconds later, "But I don't need you shitting in the driver's seat of my car. If you have stomach issues, just move to the back so you can hose it down easily afterward."

He snapped his head around to look at her, hoping to glare in just the right way that she would realize she was being ridiculous. But Valance was impervious to that, it seemed, and her blue eyes just stared back at him like, *do we have an understanding?*

So, he was forced to say it. "I don't have to … It's not stomach problems. I just didn't eat anything before work."

She sighed and returned her eyes to the dark neighborhood road. "That wasn't very smart, now was it?"

"It wasn't intentional. I just overslept."

"Ah, okay." She seemed to accept that answer without judgment. "Happens to the best of us during our rookie year. Total overload and then it's nothing but work and pass the fuck out. Especially when you work nights. You'll get used to it, though. Just takes a bit."

Either Green was losing his mind, or Valance had just said something comforting and compassionate. Maternal was not a word he'd use to describe her, but maybe there was more to her than met the eye. And if Becky was to be believed, Valance was usually nicer than this to everyone but humans and, apparently, jail nurses who stood up for humans.

It occurred to him that he didn't know anything about Valance's personal life. Was she married? He didn't remember her saying anything about a husband or wife, and she didn't wear a wedding ring. But lots of married people didn't wear wedding rings on the job. It was a practical measure to avoid tearing off a finger if the ring got hooked on a chain-link fence during a foot pursuit or a million other strange scenarios one could never dream up but had taken place to remove that particular digit. And he hadn't spoken to her about his personal life, either, come to think of it. Not that there was much to talk about. She didn't strike him as someone who gave a shit about a few short, failed relationships in a podunk human town, and he sure as shit would never tell her about Becky, even if there wasn't much to tell at this point. But when—no, if—there was more, that information was totally, one hundred percent off-limits to everyone he worked with.

"Officer Valance, do you have, like, a spouse or kids or anything?"

"Why, because I'm a woman in my thirties you assume I should have settled down by now?"

"No! That's not it at all. I just—"

"It's fine. Everyone always makes assumptions about me. In that sense, I'm glad you just came out and asked. And it only took you about a month to muster up the balls for it. That's impressive. Well, no, not impressive. More than I expected, though."

He couldn't be sure if she was insulting him or genuinely appreciative, so he kept his mouth shut and let her continue.

"The answer, and I'm sure this won't surprise you once you hear it, is that, no, I have no husband because I can't ever keep a man around and no wife because that sounds like more trouble than it's worth. I have no kids because I hate kids. There. Are we all caught up?"

"Yep." He didn't dare ask another question about her personal life, and he was spared any necessity for it as they turned onto the street where the call had come out and searched for the correct address.

Green parked in front of the driveway and they got out. As she rounded the front of the car, she said, "Prepare yourself for a tear fest, Rookie. You obviously can't understand because you're human, but this is an emotional time for a parent as it is, and to have the child run off during it only intensifies the emotion."

She spoke like she actually understood parenthood. Or emotions.

"I can kind of understand. One of my friends in high school took off when he first realized he could shift. He didn't want his family to know he was a shifter, so—"

Valance stopped in her tracks and turned to him. "Are

you expecting a hug at the end of this? Because this sounds like a story where you'll expect a hug at the end."

"Uh, no … No hug."

"Great. Then allow me to be the first woman ever to say this to you: let's wrap it up and get to the fun part." She nodded at the front door, but before she made it two yards up the driveway, an angry male voice erupted from inside, followed by a woman sobbing. Valance jogged the rest of the way and banged on the door. "Kilhaven Police! Open the door."

Green planted himself a half-step behind her on the stoop, both of them deathly silent, listening for what might be happening inside.

This was supposed to be a simple runaway call, but it was already something completely different and unknown, and Green's adrenaline kicked in immediately. He could hear the blood pulsing in his ears as he listened.

A woman's shriek followed by a thud was enough for Valance to grab the door handle, but the door didn't open. She didn't waste time. "Move back." She took a step back herself and with a well-placed kick right by the handle, knocked the door open to reveal a well-lit and by all accounts *ordinary* home inside. Maybe even a little upscale by some standards, with a nice china cabinet visible from the foyer and a high-end L-shaped sofa in the clean, organized living room to the right. It reminded Green a little of his childhood home.

Further screaming guided Valance and Green upstairs and down a short hall into the master bedroom, where a man and woman in their late forties stood arguing on either side of their king-size bed.

69

Green noted the headboard. Yep, adults definitely did the headboard thing. He'd have to look into it.

You know, after breaking up this domestic disturbance.

The man's back was to them, so it was the woman who noticed them first, a split second before Valance announced their presence loudly. "Kilhaven Police! Hands where I can see them, sir!"

Tears streamed down the woman's caramel-colored cheeks, and her thick black hair, which had been pulled back in a bun, was messy in a clearly unintentional way with long strands dangling in front of her face and loops of it poking up from her head, like something, or someone, had snagged it.

The man whirled around and stumbled back, falling onto the bed, when his eyes locked onto Valance's drawn gun and Green's drawn Taser.

"Whoa, whoa," he said, his hands in the air. "I didn't lay a hand on her!"

"He's lying!" the woman sobbed.

The man stood quickly from the bed and turned toward the woman, but he only made it a step around the bed before Valance holstered her firearm, leaped on him, and had the man in cuffs. The steel cuffs, Green noted.

The father, at least, wasn't a shifter. Man, he wished he could sniff this out like Valance could.

"*You're* calling *me* a liar?!" the man raged, despite Valance's tight hold of him. "Fifteen years, Shannon! I raised that boy as my own for fifteen years! Because I thought he *was* my own!"

And suddenly it clicked for Green.

Oh shit.

Shannon continued her sobbing, clutching herself tightly. "He is!" But she only sobbed harder then.

"Like hell he is, you cheating bitch!"

"Okay," Valance said, "time out." She forced the man to sit down on the bed. "Green, will you take her out of here?"

"Sure thing." But before he could usher the woman out of the bedroom, Valance caught his eye and mouthed, *Human*. Green nodded back curtly and then led Shannon downstairs.

He motioned for her to take a seat on the L-shaped couch in the living room and waited for her sobbing to subside enough for her to speak coherently. "Tell me what happened, ma'am."

"Junior, my son, he accidentally shifted into a peacock at the dinner table."

"Uh-huh," Green said evenly, trying to act like that wasn't fucking weird. "And then what?"

"No," she said. "You don't understand. It was his first time shifting and … he didn't even know he was a shifter. James—my husband—and I are both human."

Green nodded. "I'm sure that was frightening for your son. And then what happened?"

"Then Junior shifted into a few more things pretty rapidly—I think there was a guinea pig and a sea turtle in there, but I can't remember what else—then he shifted into a ringtail cat and ran out the cat door before we could stop him."

"And what time was this?"

"I don't know. About seven thirty, I guess. We always eat dinner at seven thirty. But it was toward the end of the meal, so maybe seven forty-five?"

Green checked his wrist watch. "Junior has been missing for about six hours now?"

She nodded. "And James hit me."

Oof. This was entering new territory, even though Green had guessed as much from the scene upstairs. He took a seat on the large ottoman in front of Shannon and pulled out a notepad and a pen from his shirt pocket. "Okay, tell me about that." He flipped to an empty page and wrote the date.

"After Junior ran off, my husband accused me of cheating on him with his best friend, who's a shifter. He called me all sorts of things, claimed he'd always suspected it, but our son's reveal was proof."

"Well, it's not unheard of for two human parents to have a paranormal son, if one or both of them have some paranormal blood in their—"

"Oh no," she said, shaking her head. "James is right. I've been fucking his best friend for almost two decades. He should have known, honestly."

Green swallowed hard. "Ah. Then what happened?"

"I told him it was true, that I'd been fucking Dante for years and that Dante was the actual father. And that the reason I'd been fucking Dante was that I couldn't stand the sight of James's tiny white cock."

Green blinked a few times, trying to process it, then scribbled it down. "Okay. I imagine he didn't take that well."

Shannon straightened her posture and ran a flat palm over her hair, trying ineffectively to smooth it down where it stuck out in all directions. "No. He didn't. He grabbed me by the hair and dragged me into our bedroom. He said he would put a baby in me with his tiny dick and then leave me."

Green sighed. "And then?"

"And then I laughed at him, and he hit me across the face."

This wasn't the first time Green had struggled with the definition of "victim" in a situation, and he was sure it wouldn't be the last. Before he could ask for further details from Shannon, a shout of "Kilhaven Police!" caught his attention and a moment later Officers Lawrence and Brooks appeared in the foyer. They nodded to Green when they spotted him. "Saw the door was kicked in," Brooks said, "and we figured we should hurry in."

Lawrence, looking put together and confident as ever, arched a thick but shapely brow and took a look around the organized home. "Don't see any fires to put out, though."

"My son is missing!" Shannon exclaimed. "You need to find him. He's scared and could run into traffic or something."

"Oh Jesus," Green said. "Yeah, I guess I hadn't thought about that."

"Okay," Lawrence said. "Any idea where he might be, ma'am?"

She nodded. "The woods behind our backyard. There's a small green space that leads down to a river. Junior goes there with his friends sometimes. I assume that's where he went, but I haven't had a chance to look."

Lawrence nodded and rolled his shoulders. "Okay. We'll start looking right away." He turned to Green. "Where's Valance?"

"Upstairs with the husband."

"Nope," came a voice from the stairs. "We're heading out to the car." She guided James ahead of her, still in cuffs.

"Green, you and Lawrence head out and look for the kid. Brooks, will you stay with Mrs. Bertrand?"

Officer Brooks rolled her eyes. "Why, 'cause I'm a woman?"

"Yes," Valance said plainly, "because you're a woman and can understand emotions better than these two oafs."

Brooks shrugged and nodded a concession then headed over to where Green sat, motioning for him to get up before taking his place on the ottoman.

If it meant excusing himself from the relationship drama, Green was more than happy to be an oaf, and he followed Lawrence to the back door and out onto the patio. "Okay, she wasn't kidding in there," Lawrence said immediately, his demeanor changing from calm and congenial to all business. "Undocumented shifters do tend to get frightened and run into traffic, and that's never good news. Human and animal parts scattered everywhere. Let's make quick work of this. Do you know what you're looking for?"

Green shook his head. "No idea, actually."

Lawrence smiled, a cocky half-grin that Green imagined was solely responsible for getting the handsome devil laid on more than one occasion, and shook a finger at him. "Exactly. You have no idea what you're looking for. Listen to your intuition. When we shifters take an animal form, we smell exactly like the animal, so you have to rely on other things. Although," he grimaced apologetically, "I guess you have to do that anyway. But hey! Maybe that'll make you better at this." He slapped Green on the back and then took off toward the fence line, hopping it with ease.

Green managed to clear the privacy fence on his third attempt. He looked around, then headed in the opposite direction that Lawrence had gone.

The woods were quiet except for the sound of cicadas, but even those seemed subdued tonight. Then it occurred to him: Junior could have shifted into a cicada. He stopped in his tracks, one foot lifted into the air. *Or an ant.* He could have already crushed the kid. But no, he would have known, because the boy would have shifted back at least a little bit upon death.

An image of crumbled human body parts and antennae flashed into Green's mind, and he flinched but shoved it away. No point in making up horrific images when the odds were good that he'd encounter horrific images without any help from his dumb imagination.

He started walking again, trying to remain quiet to listen for anything moving through the dense overgrowth.

Or he could have shifted into a bear. Fuck. That was an option, too. Or a rhino. A pissed off rhino. And then what would Green do? He looked around. None of these wimpy trees seemed thick enough to withstand the brunt of a rhino charge, should he even manage to climb one. He could shoot the beast with his silver bullets, but that was not the ideal outcome for a runaway. That would be all over the news. *Human Cop Shoots Lost, Scared Shifter Teen.* He hadn't spent all that much time in Kilhaven, but he didn't need to, to understand that this city was one unfavorably reported story away from a species-riot. And he'd be damned if he let himself be the catalyst for it.

A small rustle to his left snapped him from his gloomy thoughts, and he opened his eyes wide, willing his pupils to dilate so that he could better see what had made the noise.

Then he remembered he had a flashlight on his duty belt, and that seemed like a good thing to use in this situation. He clicked it on, and it wasn't long before the beam landed on a small skunk.

He listened for his intuition to pipe up, but mostly his mind was flooded with the hope that this wasn't his guy, that he didn't have to wrangle a frightened shifter in skunk form. Dealing with piss-soaked transients was one thing, but being sprayed would be a whole new level of unpleasant bodily fluids.

He decided to shadow the animal for a while. From Mrs. Bertrand's description of Junior's first shift, he changed forms pretty regularly. If the skunk just did skunk-like things and didn't change within a few minutes, that seemed like a solid enough sign it was just a regular skunk, and then Green could let it be.

Okay, one minute of regular skunk behavior was plenty before Green decided that, no, this was not the kid. He slowly backed away and headed in another direction.

After a few minutes of searching the empty woods, he considered heading back to the Bertrand house. There wasn't even a guarantee that the kid was still in these woods. If he'd shifted into an eagle or a cheetah he could be long gone by now, in another zip code somewhere. Why had the parents waited so many hours before calling the cops? Yet another case of irresponsible adults ruining children's lives and then doing a piss poor job of cleaning up the mess.

Something large rustled the brush to Green's left. He whirled around, aiming his flashlight in the direction of the sound. Damn, that could easily be a bear by the amount of noise it'd made. He switched the flashlight to his left hand so his right could go down to his belt, but then he reconsidered, switched the flashlight again and lowered his left hand down toward his Taser. Surely a bear could be tased, right?

He was starting to seriously doubt that a bear could be tased when something moved close to the ground. He aimed the flashlight down at it to reveal a cottontail bunny hopping from the source of the sound. A bunny? But he could have sworn whatever had been rustling around had been at least the size of a man.

Oh. That probably meant it was his shifter. Okay.

"Kilhaven Police," he said just loud enough so the bunny could hear. While it may have heard, it certainly didn't care, and it hopped back in the direction of the Bertrand home.

That worked. All Green had to do was make sure it continued on that trajectory, and then if it started to shift back into a human, he'd slap some silvers on the boy and take him in safely.

Green proceeded with caution, so as not to scare the prey and cause himself a chase that didn't need to happen and that he wasn't entirely sure he'd get the best of. Bunnies were fat, but they'd evolved solely as prey, and their only defense mechanism was hurriedly getting the hell out of Dodge when something came up on them. He remained about five feet behind it at all times—close enough to lunge for it if it decided to jet, but far enough away that all he had to do was make just a little bit of noise when it paused to get it hopping again.

The back porch light came into view. They were almost there. But fifty or so feet before the fence, the bunny took a sharp right, and before Green could adjust, it jetted.

"Fuck!" He couldn't let it get away. If he managed to be the one to catch the shifter all on his own with no help from a paranormal nose, he might actually get some respect.

Becky was right, he may not have the extra strong senses, but that just meant he didn't have to use a crutch. He could be a good cop without it, and because he was starting from a deficit, that made him a better cop than everyone else. For some reason that mattered. A lot.

The white of the cottontail's ass was an easy enough point to focus in on, and he hoped to God this boy didn't shift again into something severely dangerous right before Green could apprehend him.

"Kilhaven Police!" he whisper-shouted again, but the bunny didn't stop. It did, however, make a sharp right and head toward the house again, making straight for a small alley between the side fence of the Bertrand yard and the fence of their neighbor's yard. Maybe the boy was running home. Fine. As long as Junior made it home, that was that. Although it would be a lot better if Green could be the one to bring him in.

When the bunny paused suddenly in its spastic sprint, just at the opening between the two fences, Green stopped, too, waiting.

No, he'd waited enough.

He moved at an angle so that he approached the bunny from behind. If he could get within about five feet, he was sure he could lunge and snatch up the shifter before the teen had a chance to dart.

He stepped closer and closer, and the plan seemed to be working.

Then his radio spat out, "Fang 9-01 to 9-07, where are you?"

The bunny's head shot up, and it looked around. Now or never. Green lunged.

After only a little wriggling, the shifter gave up and

admitted defeat in Green's arms. Dopamine flooded through him. Did he put cuffs on the bunny?

Duh, no. Instead he scrambled toward the front of the house.

Officer Valance's back came into sight on the front porch just as his radio crackled again. "Fang 9-01 to 9-07, where are you?" she finished before turning around toward him, radio in hand. She cocked her head to the side slowly at the sight of Green. "Found him," she announced.

Brooks and Lawrence came into view, too, and once Valance stepped to the side, he noticed another figure on the front porch, sitting on one of the steps, a blanket around his scrawny teenage shoulders.

"I already told you no pets," Valance said, a tiny smirk visible at the corners of her mouth.

Green stopped in his tracks and felt heat rush into his cheeks as Lawrence and then Brooks caught sight of him and began laughing. He looked from the teenage boy down to the bunny in his arms. Part of him wanted to drop the dumb animal and step on its skull, but mostly he wanted to take it back out into the woods, cradle it close to his chest and have a good cry.

Neither was an option, though. Green forced himself to chuckle along with his shift mates, hoping that his suddenly upset stomach didn't make him hurl in front of everyone, and then he took the bunny back to the side yard and set it down carefully. He stood, kicked a foot at it to make it scamper off, and tried to take a few deep breaths before confronting the others again.

"Where'd you find him?" Green asked, hoping to at least steer the conversation toward something other than how he spent near an hour tracking a bunny.

"We didn't," Lawrence replied. "He just came back home."

"Usually do," Brooks added.

Lawrence nodded. "Yeah, I guess I should have mentioned that. But hey! At least if we ever need to locate a missing bunny, we know who to turn to, now!" He chuckled, and the wound was pried open a little more.

Gritting his teeth, Green swallowed down the bile that rose in his throat. He couldn't imagine Valance would show any mercy on his daily evaluation. If anything, it would likely be the most descriptive one she'd written.

Becky was right. No one respected humans on the Force. His attempt to redeem himself—and by proxy his entire species—had only plummeted him further down the food chain. Fantastic.

CHAPTER NINE_

Officer Green wasn't thrilled to be heading back out into the swampland. While the incident with the gator had been the most adrenaline-pumping of his first four weeks on the job, the few calls he'd gone to out there since weren't any less of a bad daytime TV talk show on meth.

This one, though, felt different, even in the call text that Green read on the HAM. For one, the call text had more exclamation points than usual. That was a clue. But there was also no mention of anyone's cousin or cheating. That was an aberration for sure.

The caller had heard something a trailer over that was so loud and disturbing that it was worth calling the cops. The mere idea of that sent chills down Green's spine. He read over the call text one more time as the cruiser slowed to a crawl, approaching the address listed. *"Hurry please! There was a terrible noise! A scream! I've never heard one like it! Then silence! I think someone might be—"*

The caller couldn't finish the description, and the

dispatcher had switched into reassurance mode almost immediately as he'd sent out the message.

A small figure in white appeared at the edge of the headlight's reach. "That's probably our gal," Valance said.

As they drew nearer, Green could see that the woman was getting up there in age, probably mid to late sixties, and hugged a white blanket tightly around her shoulders. She stared wide-eyed into the headlights.

"Ten bucks it's a were-deer."

Green glanced doubtfully at his FTO.

She shrugged casually. "What? That's what they do. That's why there aren't many of them around. Dumb as rats, on the whole."

Green narrowed his eyes at her. "Do you hate everyone but werewolves?" he asked before he could think better of it.

But Valance didn't react with the anger he would have expected, had he thought the question through. Instead, she chuckled lightly and glanced at him, as if he'd told a funny joke. When his face didn't match that hypothesis, she straightened her expression. "Hmm. Okay. You think I'm creaturist. Good to know."

He stopped the car and threw it into park. "No, I didn't say that."

"Yeah, you kinda did. And that's fine. But for the record" —she unbuckled and looked over at Green—"I hate werewolves, too."

The bundled woman waddled up to the car but stopped a few yards short, continuing to stare into the headlights.

"Ma'am?" Valance said. The woman didn't react. "*Ma'am?*"

"Huh?" The woman jerked her head around toward Valance and blinked a few times.

"What's your name, ma'am?" Valance asked, taking a few careful steps forward.

"Why the fuck you askin'?"

Whoa. That turned quickly. But Valance didn't flinch. "Just standard procedure, ma'am. You're not in any trouble. We just need your name."

"May."

"Full name, please?" Valance prompted.

"May You Rot In Hell."

"Oh for fu—" Valance caught herself. "Okay, Ms. Eurottenhell, were you the one who called the cops?"

"Yeah. What of it?" May pulled her blanket tighter around her shoulders.

Even from a few yards away, Green could see the sharp outline of Valance's jaw shift as she ground her teeth together. "Do you want our help or—"

A strong gust of wind blew from behind Green and Valance, and May sniffed the air sharply before taking a quick step back, her eyes wide as saucers as she stared at Valance.

"Werewolf? They sent me a goddamn werewolf?" Green saw her muscles tighten and he lunged, making a grab for her. But before he could reach her, May Eurottenhell changed in the blink of an eye, from standing on two feet to standing on four hooves, then she scampering off into the darkness between trailers, her blanket left on the ground behind her and the nightgown she wore under it bunched up around her neck.

Damn, Valance was right.

"I told you," Valance said, sighing. "Fucking were-deer.

83

Too easily startled for their own good. Almost impossible to tell a were-deer from a tweaker unless you can smell them. And even then, it's not uncommon to find tweaker were-deer."

"Do you think that's why the call text was so frantic? Because she's a tweaker? Or a were-deer? Or a tweaker were-deer?"

Valance sniffed the air. Her eyes narrowed on the home ahead of them, and she lowered her voice. "No. I don't think that's why the call text was so frantic. Follow me. It's this one right over there." They made for a small green trailer that had seen better days—and even those better days probably weren't great.

Moonlight was all they had to navigate by once the headlights of the car were blocked out by a home that was hardly more than an opaque pop tent.

Valance held up her hand for Green to stop, and boy did he. Any sign of hesitation in his FTO sent icy fear through him.

She sniffed the air. Then she drew her gun.

Green hurriedly followed suit.

Quietly she used her free hand to speak into the radio on her shoulder. "Fang 9-01 to 9-80, supervisor needed in the Shady Grove trailer park. There's a strong stench of blood coming from the address in question."

She could smell blood from ten yards away? Shit. He'd have to make sure never to miss a shower after his mornings with Becky. He'd also have to be sure to say no to burritos next time it was suggested. At least until he was off field training and had a vehicle to himself.

The front door was ajar, and it wasn't much longer until

even Green could smell something wafting from the house, but it didn't smell like blood.

"Oh God …" he moaned, and Valance whipped around with a finger to her lips.

Any more complaints he might've voiced dropped dead in his throat.

He listened, willing his ears to be anything but sucky and human, but no sounds issued from inside.

When Valance flicked on her flashlight, so did Green, just a step behind. She whipped around before entering into the putrid trailer. "Backlighting, idiot. Turn that shit off," she hissed.

Oh shit. He clicked off the flashlight. *There goes my daily tactical rating.*

They entered the trailer and Green fought the urge to hack and cough. Blood could have been raining down from the ceiling and Green didn't think he'd be able to detect its metallic scent over the smell of rotten food and—what was that, cat shit?

And once he entered the main room of the home, he discovered it had been more of an apt observation than he would have wished. Because as he stepped out from behind Valance and clicked on his flashlight, tilting it upward and he saw that blood was sort of raining down from the ceiling. Or at least it was spattered across the ceiling, and tiny droplets fell to the soggy carpet here and there. But the blood wasn't only on the ceiling and carpet. It was also on the furniture. And the boxes of whatever the fuck. And the two corpses.

Oh, holy shit! Corpses!

Only later did he realize that his first thought had been

corpses and not *victims* or *people* or anything other than the equivalent of, "Oh yeah, that's for sure dead."

And with good reason, because as he approached and the sight came into stronger relief, he noted that one of the corpses was partially shifted, his arms and legs that of a gray wolf. It was as obvious a giveaway as the deep slash marks across the human part of the torso, shredding the werewolf's clothes and staining the cloth with a deep burgundy of blood. So much blood.

Those wounds must have been the source of the spatter everywhere, because the other corpse, whose skin was deathly pale, showed no obvious or immediate signs of a cause of death—at least not as obvious as being filleted.

Unless perhaps she had died of a vitamin D deficiency?

Valance remained silent until the small house was cleared as reasonably as it could be, considering the many hiding places a trash labyrinth like this might provide for a small enough creature. Once Green had cleared his side of the trailer, which consisted of a cramped bathroom that made the ones he'd used on planes seem spacious and luxurious, and the kitchen, he met Valance back in the corpse room. He supposed it could be called a living room, but even before the owners lay dead in it and that obvious irony set in, he doubted much living could take place in it among the rot and stacked debris.

Valance leaned down over the pale corpse, shining her light straight onto the dead face.

"Human?" Green asked.

She nodded.

He shined his light onto the other. "Werewolf?"

She nodded again.

"Officer Green," she said, her voice strangely tight.

"Yes?"

"Are you seeing this?" She squatted next to the human, her beam homing in on a single spot.

He leaned over, careful to mouth breathe as he did. When he inspected the illuminated area on the corpse's neck, he realized why Valance's breathing had become shallow. "Is that what it looks like?" He looked up into her face for answers, but she wouldn't take her eyes off the twin puncture wounds.

"I believe so." She stood and breathed deeply, shutting her eyes tight and putting her hands on her head to open her lungs. "We need to be careful here."

Green only recognized the fang marks from a single slide that had gotten no more than five seconds of screen time in the academy. It had been practically an afterthought, nothing more.

"And here is what it would look like were a vampire to take a victim, but the odds are that you'll go your whole career without encountering one of these, since the Treaty of Hornstooth put an end to random attacks, as I'm sure you learned all about in eighth-grade history."

And then the instructor, Detective Bantem, had flipped to the next slide.

But the image had seared itself into Green's psyche, and now he saw it right in front of his eyes, and he had no idea what to do next.

Judging by her lack of action, neither did Valance, and that was even more disturbing than the bloodless victim lying on a pile of fast-food wrappers.

Then she took another deep breath and set her jaw the way she always did when she'd made up her mind and God help anyone who stood in her way. Usually, though, that was in regard to whether or not some drunk was going to jail, not what to do about a clear vampire killing that broke a long-standing treaty between the ruling class and the underlings.

Cool as could be, Valance radioed, "Fang 9-01 to 9-80, no backup needed except yours, and just on a technicality. Repeat, no need for additional backup, but we do have a witness who is insisting on a supervisor."

The time between the crackle of Valance's radio and Knox's response was an empty, dark space that Green could feel in his spine. But finally, Knox responded. "Fang 9-80 to 9-90, do you copy? Looks like you're closer to Shady Grove."

"Negative, 80," Valance cut in. "Witness's refusing to talk to men. She already called 9-07 a cocksucking faggot." She glanced at Green and shrugged a shoulder in a hollow apology. "Dunno what's up with her, but we need *your* assistance, 9-80."

A momentary pause then, "80 to 01. Okay. Fine. On my way. About ten minutes out."

"The wounds. The ones on the were," Green whispered, feeling it unwise to make much noise at all. "Are they vampire, too?"

Valance nodded curtly. "Most likely. My guess is the two deceased were friends, if not romantically involved, and when the suspect arrived, the werewolf tried to intervene. But there's just no competition there. Not even with a werewolf."

"I didn't know vampires had claws."

"They don't." She held up her hands. "They have nails. Gross as shit, too. Long, gangly. But not brittle. More like talons than claws. They only come out during the blood fury, though. Pray you never have occasion to see those spindly fuckers." She braced one fist on her hip and wiped a hand over her nose and mouth. "Man, it smells like balls in here." She looked around, letting her flashlight roam over the stacks. "Least the vampire could do was light this place on fire. Save someone a whole lot of clean-up and save us from finding ourselves cunt-deep in a sloppy vampire murder."

Something shiny by the werewolf's body caught Green's attention. "Hey, what's this?" He bent down close, inspecting it to discover it was a small, shiny cross. His first thought was silver, but considering it lay closer to the werewolf, he suspected it must be steel. He left it where it was, knowing better than to touch it.

Valance squatted down, interested until he showed her what he was looking at. "Oh," she said. "This shit never works. Vampires don't give two fucks about crosses. But that doesn't stop these uneducated, sludge-brained muckers from perpetuating the myth. You want to keep a vampire away? Move within two hundred yards of a school. That's about the only place even the most inbred vamps know they're not allowed." She kicked the cross with her steel-toed boot, and it skittered across the carpet and onto the browned linoleum floor of the kitchen, landing somewhere behind a stack of unlabeled VHS tapes.

The sound of tires crunching gravel outside preceded the flash of beams across the front side of the trailer, lighting up the dark drapes. "Finally," Valance breathed. She turned to Green. "Knox is the only one with half a chance of taking this seriously. But only if you keep your mouth shut and let me handle it. She and I go way back, and for obvious reasons, she takes it personally whenever a paranormal kills a human."

"Obvious reasons?" Green asked.

Valance exhaled sharply and rolled her eyes. "Really? You're that scent blind? She's a human, Green. Just like you."

"Oh. No, I knew that," he lied. He could tell Valance knew it was a lie, too, but she let it be, heading toward the open front door. She paused and looked over her shoulder. "Don't let them out of your sight. I'll be right back."

But Knox was already there at the door before Valance could step outside, and the FTO held up a hand to stop the corporal before she could get a clear look of the interior. "Remember what I told you about on our last hike?"

Knox paused, cocking her head slightly to the side and looking incredibly unsure of herself. "You mean the double-ended dil—"

"No. Not that. The other thing. The work-related thing."

It took a moment, but then comprehension seemed to dawn on Knox. "Wait. Here?"

Valance stepped to the side. "See for yourself."

Knox inhaled deeply, her chest puffing up before she took a few bold strides toward the scene where Green stood watch. The air whooshed from her lungs when she looked down at the victims. "Oh geez …"

Valance's eyes flickered to meet Green's, then she folded her arms over her chest and stood stock still while Knox squatted down to inspect the bodies.

"Green," Valance said, "show her the bite mark."

He did as instructed, shining his flashlight onto the human's neck wounds.

Knox examined them closely, then slid on a pair of gloves and leaned down, gently poking at one of the two punctures, and as she did so, a royal purple liquid began to ooze from it.

Next, Knox shifted her weight to lean over the werewolf, who'd so far gotten the least attention of the two corpses. She placed her pointer and middle finger into one of the slices of the were's filleted flesh then moved them apart, separating the wound further and causing a new bit of fresh crimson to bubble out where the drying, clotted blood cracked open.

"It's definitely recent," she remarked. "Even though you wouldn't be able to tell by the human." She sighed and then rose to standing, looking around the dank room and shaking her head.

When her eyes landed on Valance, she said, "Listen, I know what you think this is. But I also know that you've become a little, I dunno, fixated on that lately. It could be a lot of things."

"Bullshit," Valance rasped.

"No," Knox said more forcefully, clearly trying to assume the corporal role over that of Valance's friend and hiking buddy, "it's not necessarily bullshit. I could call up Sarge, tell him we have a, you know, situation on our hands before we fully investigate this, or I could wait to stir the pot, and we can all hope for the sake of our careers that this is something else entirely. Personally, I think the second option sounds like the best, don't you, Green?"

Both women turned to look at him, and he wondered if there were a way to move his head at such an angle that from where Valance stood more to his right, it looked like he was shaking it and from where Knox stood just to his left, it would look like he was nodding. He gave it a shot, bobbing his head up and down and side to side in a strange zigzagging circle until both women just ignored him and got back to their discussion.

"Look." Knox leaned over the werewolf. "These claw marks could be from a bear, right?"

Valance rolled her eyes. "I suppose."

"So, we could have either a bear shifter or a were-bear as a suspect." She stepped over the wolf and now leaned over the human. "And these puncture wounds look a little like fang marks, right?"

"Yeah, vampire fa—"

A muscle to the side of Knox's mouth flinched, and she held up a hand to halt Valance. "We *don't know that*. I'd say a very large snake could leave these bite marks as well. You could be dealing with a were-snake—"

"Not a thing," Valance interjected.

"Or a snake shifter. Just find the common denominator here, and it's a shifter, which works out as a more plausible scenario because Shady Grove is almost entirely shifters. I'm surprised two non-shifters ended up in the same building."

Valance shut her eyes and massaged at her temples. "Diane, I know you've worked your ass off to make it to corporal as a human, and I know you don't want to jeopardize your career to expose a breach of Hornstooth, but I'm a little bit surprised at you here. What you just proposed is easily the dumbest shit I've heard all week. And I have a rookie with me, so that's saying something." She opened her eyes to glare at the corporal. "You're telling me that you think a shifter came in here, shifted into a bear, killed the wolf, and then, what? Shifted into an anaconda and killed the human?"

"Why not?"

"Glad you asked. First off, what was the human doing

while the shifter was taking on the were? Second of all, an anaconda would have to wrap up its victim to hold it steady, and there's no sign of that sort of crushing pressure on him. Trust me, I know the signs of an anaconda—"

"I know, I know." Knox waved off Valance. "You saw it in South America." She paused. "You know, Heather, it's almost like you *want* this to be a vampire killing."

Green wasn't sure which left him more anxious, Knox saying the words "vampire killing" or Knox calling Valance by her first name like a friend would another.

"It's the last thing I want, and you know it." Valance's shoulders stiffened and she braced her hands on her duty belt. "I'm just not too chickenshit to call it like it is when the devil comes knocking. That's why I managed to survive Nicaragua and Ecuador and all those other shitholes to come home and work in the smelliest shithole of them all. And you still haven't explained the blood draining," she finished with a curt nod, reining herself back in.

Knox had clearly had enough. "You know you don't get to tell me what to do, Officer Valance. I've got rank on you."

Valance lifted up her hands defensively. "I know. I just wish you would sack up and start acting like it."

Knox's lips pressed together into a thin line, and she huffed out air through her nose. As her attention wandered back down to the two bodies for a moment, something in her seemed to give way, some small cord of hope snapping. "God dammit. Sarge is not going to like this." She pulled off her gloves inside out and stuffed them in her pants pocket. "God fucking dammit." Then she grabbed her radio off her shoulder. "Fang 9-80 to 9-90 over in Shady Grove trailer park. I need you over here stat."

Valance nodded, but she didn't seem happy, even though

she'd won the argument. "Sorry, Diane," she breathed. "But it's the right call."

"I know. That's why I did it. And fuck you, by the way."

Valance was unmoved. "It just takes a few people in our position to ignore something like this for the balance of a city to tip in the wrong direction."

"I said fuck you, Heather, and I meant it." Then Corporal Knox stomped from the trailer.

Valance watched her go then patted Green between the shoulder blades. "As long as we don't all get fired for this, you might just pass your final eval, Rookie."

CHAPTER TEN_

Green was settling into the meetings at the start of each shift just like everyone on his shift seemed to settle into the idea of seeing him there. Did that mean they were accepting him as part of the shift, despite his species? Sure, Corporal Knox was a distinguished member of the shift *now*. But certainly it'd taken more than Green's measly five and a half weeks before they'd fully accepted her as one of their own.

It was almost time for the meeting to start, where Sergeant Montoya would run through any ongoing situations in Fang sector and flash around the latest BOLOs for the officers to study. Green's stomach jumped inside him at the thought of seeing Sergeant Montoya. He hadn't been able to sleep that day partly because he couldn't stop thinking about how angry and tense the sarge looked when he'd arrived on scene at Shady Grove trailer park the night before. (But, admittedly, some of his sleep deprivation was also owed to Becky's early morning booty call that had eaten well into Green's usual sleeping hours of seven in the morning till five in the afternoon.)

In the gravel of Shady Grove, outside the gore-filled trailer, Corporal Knox had made it clear to the sergeant that she intended to include suspicion of vampire involvement in her report. He'd gruffly attempted to dissuade her, and there was a moment when Green thought the corporal might actually cave, but with Valance's stern glares to urge her on, Knox had stood her ground.

And that's how things were left with Sergeant Montoya, with him standing there red-faced but resigned, observing the scene with his clear sense of unease and occasionally casting looks of suspicion and mistrust at Valance and Green, like they were complicit in some conspiracy he felt but couldn't yet unravel.

When Valance sauntered into the shift meeting, a large coffee in her hand, she looked as relaxed as Green had ever seen her.

But the mere sight of Valance caused panic to rise in Green's chest as he had to reassure himself that, yes, he had showered since he parted with Becky earlier that afternoon, and yes, he'd remembered to put on extra cologne just in case. The situation with the nurse had become almost a daily rendezvous, and Green wondered how long he could keep it up before word got out. Considering the unthinkable things Becky had done to him the night before, he planned on keeping at it until somebody *made* him stop. For a woman who apparently couldn't read his mind, Becky seemed to be able to read his mind.

Valance took a seat next to him with a small conspiratorial nod that almost looked like respect. He returned the gesture as confidently as he could.

Sergeant Montoya cleared his throat and started the rattling old projector, jumping straight into the BOLOs.

It must be a slow night if we're skipping straight to BOLOs.

"Forrest Smith, age nineteen—"

"Shouldn't we wait for Corporal Knox before we get started?" Valance asked.

Montoya turned his head only halfway toward Valance and let his eyes traverse the rest of the distance in their sockets. "Uh, no. We'd … we'd never get started." He sighed, which sounded more like a low snuff of a bull then he folded his hands in front of him, the projector clicker still gripped in one, and faced the shift. Green had heard through the grapevine that Sergeant Montoya was a were-bison, and that had instantly made good sense, considering the man's build. "Corporal Knox has been suspended indefinitely."

Valance jumped to her feet, and she wasn't alone in her shock. Green felt his heart drop in his chest, and the rest of the shift murmured their surprise, too.

Montoya held up a hand to silence the officers. "I know, I know. She was very well liked around here. It's a shame to see her go."

"With all due respect, Sarge, this is bullshit."

He raised his palms defensively. "I know. Trust me. I hate to see her leave more than anyone."

"Do you?" Green had only heard that level of vitriol in Valance's voice once, and it was while they were interviewing a human who had just beaten his faun wife to death's doorstep.

Sergeant Montoya's mouth fell open just the slightest bit. "Of course! You think I had something to do with it?"

"Awfully defensive, Sergeant."

He pressed his lips together and his nostrils flared. "That's enough, Officer Valance. You may be a veteran here, but I'm your commanding officer, and I watch out for my shift. I would never hang out one of my own to dry." He narrowed his dark eyes on her, his heavy brows pulling toward the bridge of his nose. He was trying to convey a clear message to Valance, obviously, but what it was, Green couldn't be sure.

"Then why was she fired? Oh, sorry, *suspended indefinitely.*"

"She has not been fired. She's just suspended indefinitely due to an investigation into inappropriate conduct with a lower ranking officer."

Valance chuckled dryly and crossed her arms over her chest before leaning back against the table. "Oh bullshit, Sergeant. You know Knox was by the books and more ethical than any sane officer should be. If you're implying she had some sort of affair with another officer, that's just ridiculous."

Montoya cocked his head to the side, paused, then with restraint in his voice added, "The officer in question was very clear that he and Knox had an ongoing—"

"Hmph!" Valance interrupted before he could finish. "Okay, now I know it's bullshit, Sarge. But fine, fine. Go ahead with the BOLOs." She waved him onward with a flick of her wrist before folding her arms again.

Being told what to do was not one of Montoya's favorite activities—probably why he had decided to rise in the ranks —and Valance barking an order at him left him momentarily speechless with rage. But since carrying on was what he'd clearly wanted to do the whole time, he was forced to do as Valance said. He turned back to the projection.

"Smith Forrester—"

"Forrest Smith," Officer Brooks corrected politely. But even she seemed pissed in a sweetly poisonous way.

"That's what I said. Forrest Smith, age nineteen ..."

As the sergeant continued, Valance glanced over at Green. Her expression was equally as conspiratorial as before, but there was no smile there now, and on the whole, it was a foreboding expression that made Green wonder what other career paths might be possible for him once people found out about him and Hellstrom and he was immediately suspended indefinitely.

Well, he was trained in cleaning up bodily fluids now, so maybe a janitor would work. It wasn't ideal, but people mostly left the janitor alone, right? It seemed a solitary practice, good for long meditative bouts while scrubbing toilets.

By the time the meeting was concluded, Green was fairly certain that he could live a *happier* life as a janitor than as a cop, but here he was, a cop, doomed to clean up people's messes, like a janitor, but also blamed for making all the messes in the first place. At least no one accused the janitor of being the one who vomited in the hallway or pooped in the water fountain. And the news didn't care to coach from the bench on how janitors did their jobs, either.

Green made to leave, but Valance grabbed his bicep and told him to wait. She'd been oddly silent through the rest of the meeting, and Green thought that maybe she'd decided to let the Knox thing go.

No, Valance wouldn't do that. He'd *hoped* she would, though. Valance waited to allow the rest of their shiftmates to head out to the lot to finish loading up the cars, and when Montoya caught sight of what she was doing, he tried to dash out with the rest, but she cut him off and stared him down. "Was it you?" she asked bluntly.

"Was what me, Officer?"

"Was it you who suggested to some anonymous male officer that he should claim Knox had a sexual relationship with him or does this go higher up than you?"

Montoya shifted on his heels. "I know you two were close, and it won't be the same without her—"

"God dammit, Victor," she growled. He took a half-step back, and his domineering posture shrank slightly. "Just tell me. Was it you?"

He stared into her eyes for a moment, inspecting her. Then, "No, it wasn't me. I promise you, Heather."

She stepped closer to him so that their noses were only inches apart. Her above-average height for a woman put her on equal ground with Montoya, and her next words came out hardly above a whisper, as the most terrifying words usually do. "Because you know my family could put you out of a job, right?"

He said nothing, just pressed his lips together till they turned white.

Valance continued. "But I wouldn't even need to call on them to put you out of a job, Montoya. You're good at your job, and I actually like you sometimes. But I swear to all things good if you were responsible for starting this rumor about Knox that lost her job—a rumor, I might add, that we both know is false for obvious reasons—I will make sure you don't set foot in this substation again."

Montoya's top lip curled. "Are you threatening me, Heather?"

She shook her head. "Of course not." Then she backed away, turned, and made for the lot. Green, not having the least bit of desire to remain in the room with a furious were-bison, followed as closely behind Valance as he could without stepping on the heels of her boots.

While the thought of Valance being so angry that she lost control was terrifying, it turned out that seeing Valance become so enraged that she was *extra* in control was worse.

She moved with machine-like efficiency as she loaded up the car with their equipment for the night—sledgehammer, riot helmet, heavy duty vest in case some slack-jawed idiot decided to bust out the heavy artillery, and bleach for when someone inevitably pissed, shit, or vomited in the back seat.

Once the rest was in, not a word spoken by either Valance or Green, they scooted into the car in their usual spots—Green driving, Valance in shotgun.

After completing his daily check of the lights and sirens, he slowly steered the car out of the lot and onto the road.

"If I tell you something, can I trust that it just stays between us?" Valance asked.

"Like a secret?"

"No shit like a secret. I don't even know why that has to be clari— Dammit, Green, you're already making me regret this."

"No, no," he said hurriedly. "You can tell me. I promise I won't tell, and you know not even a telepath can get it out of me."

She nodded pensively. "That's one of the reasons I like humans as friends."

"You have friends?" Green asked, when what he meant to ask—would have asked if he hadn't blurted out the words as a knee-jerk reaction—was, *did she really like humans*? It seemed out of line with everything he knew about her.

"Of course I have friends, you dickhead. Now do you want to hear what I have to say or not?"

"Yes. Sorry."

She sighed as they pulled up to a red light down the

street from the sub. "I don't normally go spreading around people's business, but this seems important, and I don't know if you quite realize the shit we almost stepped in the other night. We only missed it because Knox took it upon herself to file the report.

"But I knew the minute Montoya started speaking about the anonymous male officer that whatever was being pinned to Knox was a whole heaping pile of nuh-uh."

"Why's that?" Green asked hesitantly.

"Knox is a stone-cold lesbian. I mean, that woman *loves* the vag. If there were a vag equivalent of a sommelier, she would hold that distinction, no question."

Green accidentally hit the brake pedal, and the car rocked forward midway through the intersection. "Corporal Knox?"

"Yep. But she doesn't want it to get out because she's married to a man or whatever. And no one ever suspects it because she's small and pretty and most every straight male officer in the department fantasizes about her calling him daddy and begging for him to discipline her."

"For the record," Green said, "I've never fantasized about that."

Valance frowned and glanced over at him. "Then you're an idiot. Hell, I've probably fantasized about that at some point. Doesn't matter. The point is that there's no way Knox would have an affair with any man in this department. She only has sex with her husband because he's rich as hell and she likes his money. As someone who's boned more broke, shitty lovers than I care to admit, I can't fault her for that. At least she was getting something out of it."

Green nodded along, but his brain was busy trying to

unfurl the riddle of *is Valance a lesbian?* that had long since lingered in the back of his mind.

"You know what that means, right?" the FTO asked.

Green forced his mind back to the matter at hand. "Huh? Um. It means that Montoya is lying."

Valance nodded. "Yep. I don't think he was the one who set her up, but he knows damn well it's a lie. He might be the only one in the department who knows about her preferences besides me—and now you—and only because he was her FTO when she started and he pulled out every trick in the bag to fuck her. But each one failed. She eventually got so sick of the harassment that she told him the truth. And even then, he didn't believe her, so she said if he tried anything again, she'd file a complaint. That put a stop to it."

Green nodded. Things were starting to make sense now. "How do you know all this?"

"Hikes, Rookie. You can learn a lot about another person when you spend a day a week alone in the woods with them."

Okay, that was a tally mark in the gay column.

Stop focusing on that!

"You think that someone got Knox fired because …"

"Because she filed a report about the vampire killing. She crossed a line, and someone up in the chain of command couldn't risk keeping her around knowing she was an ethical kamikaze. And maybe they wanted to send a message to us, and to anyone else who might've had eyes on the report. Probably people in homicide, definitely Montoya. I wouldn't be surprised if he got his ass chewed for even letting that report come through."

As Green's thoughts wandered down that path, Valance

said, "Yeah, of course, Sophie. That's great. No, I could use a ghost call right now. We're on it."

"Did we just assign?" Green asked.

Valance swiveled the HAM toward him and pointed at the call description. *Domestic disturbance, female poltergeist on male shifter.* He recognized the street name, which was a relief—at least he was starting to learn.

He pulled a quick U-turn and headed toward the address.

"We're gonna have to watch our ass on this, Green."

"Really? It's just a ghost."

"No, not that. But also, it's a poltergeist, not a ghost. Big difference as you're about to find out. That's not what I mean, though. I mean with the vampire. You and I were there. Whoever sacrificed Knox to get their message across and avoid dealing with reality has their eye on us. Whatever you do, act like nothing has changed. And if anyone asks you, it was a shapeshifter that went from bear to anaconda to—" She clamped her eyes shut and sighed, pinching at the bridge of her nose. "No, fuck it, it's too dumb even to say out loud. Just don't say anything about a vampire. Don't even say the word vampire. And whatever you do, keep your nose clean and don't give IA a single crumb to pick up your scent."

"Of course," Green said. "I'm not an idiot." He turned his attention back to the road as they turned onto the street for the poltergeist call.

Okay, maybe I should cancel with Becky tomorrow morning.

CHAPTER ELEVEN_

When they pulled up to the address listed on the screen, the caller and presumed victim was already outside, sitting in the driveway with an ice pack on his head. Green and Valance exited the vehicle, leaving the lights flashing but the siren off.

"Mr. Chang?" Valance called out as they headed up to where the man sat.

He had his legs stretched out in front of him, spread slightly apart, his back slumped. Something about the way he had plopped down with so little thought given to his posture, reminded Green of a sad, chastised child.

"Yes sir." Mr. Chang squinted through the dark. "Oh, I mean ma'am."

"Sir is fine," she said as Mr. Chang slowly got to his feet, grimacing with every slight movement of his head. Green stepped forward to assist the victim, and in return, Mr. Chang flashed a grateful smile.

In the last few seconds before pulling up to the Chang residence, Green had wondered how Valance would be able to handle a situation as delicate as domestic violence when she was still so full of rage at Montoya. But when she spoke, there was that strange softness in her voice that always took him aback when he heard it on calls, a kind of sterile compassion that might not have implied *"tell me about your feelings,"* but exuded safety and security, maybe even a little serenity.

"Tell me, Mr. Chang," Valance murmured, "what'd you do to piss her off?"

Green's head whipped around to see if his FTO was serious. There'd been nearly an entire week of the academy dedicated to speaking with victims of crime, almost two full days specifically focused on victims of domestic violence. Maybe Valance needed a refresher, because blaming the vic for bringing it on himself was not on any of the projector slides Green could remember.

He jumped in. "I think what she means to say—"

"Nope," Valance interrupted. "I meant what I said. What'd you do to piss her off?" The safety in her tone was slipping away quickly, like massive cracks appearing in a helipad one was just about to land on.

When the man didn't immediately answer—apparently, he was as shocked by the question as Green—she followed up with, "What was it, a toaster?" She motioned at the shifter's head where he still held the ice pack.

"Yeah," he said, dazed, "how'd you know?"

"I've seen this situation before, Mr. Chang, and the toaster is the go-to. It's located in the kitchen, where the majority of attacks happen because your back is usually toward the room as you stand at the counter. The toaster is plugged into a power source, which makes for speedy energy gathering for poltergeist manifestation, and it's a small enough shape to easily manipulate while also being large enough to leave a mark." She nodded, all business. "Your poltergeist is a smart one. Now I ask you again: what'd you do to piss her off?"

"Nothin'!" he shouted, full of indignation. "I ain't done nothin'! She just gets a wild hair up her ass about nothin' and then starts coming after me! I've told her to get out, but she won't."

Valance sighed and appeared to be losing her patience. "Okay, that's all bullshit. Will you invite us inside, Mr. Chang, so we can speak with her?"

His face went pale and slack. "You're not vampires, are you?"

"What?" Green said. "No."

Valance's upper lip curled. "Do we look like a couple of registered sex offenders to you? No, we're goddamn cops. Jesus. We just need you to give permission to enter your domicile for legal purposes. But honestly, it was more of a courtesy, since I could easily articulate a reasonable suspicion of imminent threat and enter without your blessing."

Valance was taking things too far too fast. Even for her, this was out of line. When she talked to suspects this way, it was almost enjoyable, but to speak with a victim like this was just too far for Green to stomach. "Um, Officer Valance, could I have a word?"

"Yes," she said, standing her ground.

"Er, over there?" He nodded in a general "away from the victim" direction.

"No, Officer, I think we're good here."

Shit. He never won these sorts of standoffs with women, and he definitely wouldn't win it with Valance. While he didn't want to do this in front of the victim, there didn't seem to be another option. And who knew, maybe it would help Mr. Chang to see someone standing up for him. "Uh, okay. I just think Mr. Chang has been through an ordeal and it's not right to place the blame for the incident on his actions."

The corners of Valance's mouth twitched, and a low chuckle rumbled in her chest. "Yeah, okay. I tell you what, you go interview the poltergeist inside and I'll stay out here with the *victim* and make amends." She turned to Mr. Chang. "That alright? Can Officer Green enter your home to speak with the spirit?"

Perhaps due to the head injury, Mr. Chang nodded. "Yeah, that's fine."

Green headed toward the front door and Valance hollered after him, "Don't forget to have the vengeful spirit sign the statement, Rookie."

"Right."

Wait. Vengeful spirit?

It's probably just a generic term. Man up.

The truth was, Green knew next to nothing about ghosts. If he had to name a single blind spot in his education, that would be it. Growing up, he'd thought there was a ghost down in the basement, but once he'd finally vocalized that to his mother one night, she'd laughed airily and said, "Oh no, honey. When a ghost takes up residence, there's no maybe about you. You *know*. And trust me, we don't have a ghost. At least not yet." And then she'd tucked him into bed and turned off the light.

The academy hadn't been much more helpful about ghosts. Their coverage of the topic basically consisted of one slide—a picture of a wispy white blob hovering in front of a fireplace—and the creature studies instructor saying, "They never do come out right in photos, do they? Eh, well. You probably all know the basics on ghosts anyway. And if you don't, it's not like we'll get sued for excessive use of force since they're already dead. Just do what you think is best." Then they'd moved along to a series of slides on humans, all of which Green felt were a little biased and not entirely accurate.

Before entering the Chang residence, Green took a mental inventory of everything on his duty belt. Did he remember to pop the vial of holy water into one of the pouches? He let his hand slide down to flip open a snap and reach inside. Yep. There it was. Well, that was good, at least. Outside of holy water, he didn't have much he could use against a spirit, and even the holy water wasn't much. In fact, it might only be effective if the spirit decided to possess someone, and he hoped that wasn't the case. But he wasn't even certain how to tell if it *did* become the case.

Damn, he knew nothing about ghosts.

The home was lit by dim lamps placed in the corners of each room. It reminded him of a dorm room in its hodgepodge of decor—cheap blankets with vaguely Indian patterns tacked to the wall, stuffed pillow on the floor in place of seating, a dusty radio propped up on a stack of big-screen TV boxes.

He crept around the one-story house, making sure there was no one else inside—besides the poltergeist, obviously. Once it was clear, he knew what came next in standard procedure, but something about knowing he was in a haunted house triggered a whole heap of his childhood anxieties, and shouting seemed like the last thing any intelligent person would do. But he did it anyway.

"Kilhaven Police. I need to speak with the ghost of the house."

He scanned the living room, where he'd circled back around, but there was no shimmery mist. He headed slowly into the kitchen, his gun drawn for no reason he would be able to articulate in a report.

The kitchen was where the attack had happened, so maybe it was a favorite hangout of the poltergeist. It was worth a try.

The moment he crossed the living room to the kitchen, what little muggy heat was in the air vanished, leaving him bone cold, his breath clouding in front of his face.

Okay, that probably meant he was in the right room.

"Put down the gun."

The scratchy whisper of the voice came from behind him, and he whipped around to find a mostly translucent figure sitting in a bathrobe at the metal kitchen table in the corner. She smoked a cigarette, even in the afterlife, and Green thought that was probably the best anti-smoking ad he'd ever seen. Talk about a habit you can't kick.

"Or just point the damn thing at me," she said sarcastically, but there was a menace in her voice that he could hear, even through the wobbly tone. It was like she was speaking to him through a silent waterfall that muted and garbled her words, though not so much that the meaning was lost.

He lowered his weapon and rested his hand on his belt, right next to the pouch of holy water.

"Miss …?"

"Mrs. Chang."

"Oh." This was suddenly more complicated. "Are you the sister of Mr. Chang?" he asked hopefully.

"Deceased wife of that lethally stupid slob."

Green nodded, and Mrs. Chang motioned with her hand at the chair across the table from her. "Have a seat, Officer."

"Ah, thank you, ma'am. Officer Green." He pulled out the chair and sat, despite the temperature being even less hospitable this close to her. "I'm here on a complaint by your husband that you assaulted him with a toaster."

"Yes, I did that." She took a long drag off the cigarette and exhaled a whoosh of arctic chill across the tabletop at Green.

While he could still see the wall through her, there was almost a color to her appearance. Most of the color seemed heavily implied, though. The mist of her hair heavily implied that it was dark brown. The large roses on her bathrobe heavily implied that they were pink, and the swelling around her eye heavily implied black and blue. But it was like staring at a star in the night sky; you had to look just to the side of it for your eye to really see it. While Green stared at her swollen eye, it appeared white mist, allowing her hair room to strongly imply brown.

"Are you going to cuff me?" She held out her ghastly wrists, and Green stared down at them.

"I don't think it would work if I tried."

She chuckled and shook her head. "No, it wouldn't. Even if you could bind me somehow, you wouldn't be able to take me from this house."

"I don't need to take you anywhere just yet, Mrs. Chang. Just tell me what happened, and we can sort this out."

She leaned back in the chair, going slightly through it—Green suspected this was unintentional—and inspected him under dark, heavily implied eyelashes. "Shall I start at the beginning?"

"Please do."

"Wonderful." A smirk curled her lips. "When Charlie and I were married, and I was still alive, of course—you know, before death did us part—we were so in love. He worked out of town on the weekends, and every time he came home, he would bring me a new record from an artist he thought I would love. And he was almost always right." Her eyes glistened at either the memory or because the lamplight reflected from the mist that way. "The point is that we were in love. So in love. Ten years went by, and even though he couldn't have children, we made it work." She puffed her cigarette. "And this is where the story turns, Officer Green. You ready for it?"

Green nodded and suppressed a shiver as the air around him dropped a few more degrees.

"Well, it turned out that Charlie was not, in fact, convinced that he was sterile, no matter what the doctors said. Apparently, he assumed it was *me* who couldn't have children, blaming my defective genes as a human. He became more hostile, started his collections, as he liked to call them, but it was just hoarding. And I tolerated it, because I thought he was depressed, and any loving wife tolerates that sort of behavior in light of depression. I, at least, was serious about the death do us part clause of our marriage. Little did I know that Charlie was conducting his fertility experiments whenever I left the house for work.

"One day I come home early—you see where this is going, Officer?"

Green sighed and nodded. He could *feel* where it was going too, the chill in the room almost intolerable now.

"Good. I come home early to find Charlie shagging someone in our marriage bed. I mean going to town on her doggy style—spanking, grunting, partially shifted—the whole shebang, literally. He doesn't hear me open the door, and at first, I'm too stunned to say anything, so I watch. Then I erupt, shouting and crying.

"He finally realizes I'm there, but I suppose he'd shifted his manhood into something beastly, so when he tries to pull out, he can't. The girl starts thrashing around beneath him in pain, and that's when I realize: it's our neighbor. She probably isn't a day over fifteen."

Green swallowed hard. This call had just taken a serious turn. He pulled out the pad of paper and a pen from his breast pocket. "Just gonna take some notes, Mrs. Chang."

She grinned. "Oh, be my guest. Shall I go on?"

"Yes, ma'am."

"Excellent. Once he could pull his filthy cock free, he started blaming me, saying it was my fault we couldn't have kids, and now I was too old, and there was no hope, he was going for more fertile lands, and blah blah blah. Then he went on to say maybe if I let him shift inside me, he wouldn't have the urges he did. I told him I was going to call the cops on him for raping a young girl, and when I turned to leave, I tripped over a stack of empty water bottles —one of his many 'collections'—and fell face first into the door frame." She motioned to her eye. "And then I fell onto a small pile of Hindu statues that he kept along the wall in the hallway, one of which did me the courtesy of puncturing through my skull and ending my life." She turned so that Green could see the back of her head, where the dried blood and skull fragments in her hair from the fatal injury were heavily implied.

"Jesus Christ," he whispered.

"No, I believe it was Ganesh that I landed on. Not a

terrible God to land on, if I do say. Hindus believe he's the remover of obstacles, and I might agree." She puffed on the cigarette as Green finished up his notes.

He looked up at her and sighed. "Mrs. Chang, I'm sorry that happened to you."

"It's terrible, isn't it?"

Green nodded. "So terrible." The room grew colder.

"Be honest with me, Officer Green. Would you say I deserved that treatment?"

Green shook his head adamantly as he scribbled down the rest of his notes. "Absolutely not. No one deserves that, especially a wife as dedicated as you were." As a forceful shiver ran down his spine, he wondered if the refrigerator might be a nice place to warm up at this point. Was the cold just getting to him more, or was it actually getting *colder*?

"Ma'am, did you ever get a chance to report his sexual conduct with a minor to the authorities?"

She shook her head. "Nope. Died before I could. And that was just last week."

"Oh, wow." For some reason, he had imagined her death happening years ago, but this was still fresh. "I see why you would still be upset."

"Oh yes. Very pissed. For a while, I didn't know what to do, since part of coming back as a ghost means being tied to a single person or place. As I couldn't very well get the authorities, I was stuck here, watching day after day as our teenaged neighbor skipped school, snuck over here, and let my husband roughly rape her. Today was the first time I was able to lift an object successfully. What a thrill. I discovered it right around the time Charlie's child lover arrived with a nice fertile friend to join in on the fun."

Green knew he should keep a poker face, but *holy fucking shit*. "Valance," he said into his radio, "I need you in here."

"Oh good!" Mrs. Chang said. "Backup."

"Ma'am, do you know your neighbor's name?"

"Well of course. I've only had to hear my husband growl it during intercourse every day since my untimely death. It's Jennifer. Jennifer Macintyre. Blonde hair, blue eyes, no pubic hair …"

Green paused from his notes to look up toward the ceiling and breathe in the frigid air, trying to collect himself. He could practically feel the anger and resentment coming off Mrs. Chang in waves, like everything that had happened to her had actually happened to him. His lungs felt like piss-filled balloons. He had half a mind to go outside and shake Charlie Chang until the man shit himself.

"Tell me again," Mrs. Chang said, "how wronged I've been."

Something in her voice was different now. The soft, smooth wobble sounded scratchier, deeper, more menacing. Green looked down from the spot of water damage in the ceiling he'd fixated on and leaped up from his seat when he saw what was in front of him where Mrs. Chang had just been.

Whatever was there would be difficult to articulate in the report, he knew that immediately. It was less translucent than Mrs. Chang, but more gangly, especially in the appendages, which extended farther out than Mrs. Chang's arms had, ending in claws. The head had the same brown hair as before, except less of it, and it hung down in strings, a few covering her face as fangs glistened in her open mouth.

While it bore some striking similarities to the woman

Green had just been interviewing, he might have concluded it was not, in fact, the same creature, were it not for the damning evidence of a cigarette butt in the shimmery monster's left claw. That pretty much summed it up.

"Whatever you do," came a familiar voice from the kitchen doorway, "do not validate her feelings, Officer Green."

He risked a quick look to see Valance standing there, the vial of holy water already in hand.

Returning his eyes to the poltergeist sitting at the table, he said, "But Valance, you didn't hear her story. She got a raw deal with—"

Mrs. Chang stood, and at the same time, the table and all the chairs lifted from the ground, hovering a foot above where they should've been.

"Time to go, Green," Valance said, urgency in her voice. "You screwed the pooch on this, and now it's time to call in the experts."

He backed away slowly from Mrs. Chang and toward Valance. "She didn't deserve to die, though ..." He didn't understand why he was saying it, only that he felt the sentiment so deeply he couldn't *not* say it.

A gust of warm wind blew against Green's back, knocking him forward toward Mrs. Chang as if all the air in the house were being sucked into the kitchen. A second later every single object in that room that wasn't held down by bolts and screws found itself suspended in midair. Mrs. Chang screeched, "I have the moral high ground!"

"Oooo-kay. Time to go. She's about to vent." Valance grabbed Green's arm and tugged him away from the escalating scene in the kitchen.

They'd hardly made it past the threshold of the front

door when a massive crashing sound like an avalanche boomed behind them, and a blast of icy air whooshed out on their backs, almost taking Green's feet out from under him.

Valance took off at a sprint, so *shit yeah* Green did too. Had he ever run a twenty-meter dash as fast in his life? He didn't suspect so.

Since Valance didn't stop running until she made it to the safety of the other side of the cruiser, neither did Green.

Another police vehicle was there now, too, and Green squinted over to see Charlie Chang in the backseat and Officer Lawrence staring up at the house with his ruggedly handsome jaw hanging slightly open. Then he turned to look at Green and Valance where they crouched.

Valance didn't seem to notice, instead focusing on her radio, sounding calm and collected as she said, "Fang 9-01 on scene of the domestic dispute involving a poltergeist. The situation has escalated and we could use the Stubborn Hauntings Unit out here asap."

Valance looked up at the house again just as something shiny and gold came crashing out of one of the windows. It was thrown with such force that it landed all the way across the yard, coming to a skittering stop in the street about ten feet from Green. He crawled closer and realized it was a small statue of an elephant, except the hat on the elephant's head was darkened with a dried brown liquid. Blood.

That was probably useful evidence, but it could wait to be bagged until the commotion died down a bit.

"Okay, Green, school is in session." Valance leaned her back against the tire and turned her head toward the rookie. "When a spirit of any kind starts telling its story, you can hear it out, but whatever you do, do not validate its feelings."

"But she was the victim, and with victims—"

"*Of course* she was the victim. Didn't I call that from the start? You know, before you scolded me for being insensitive? Ninety-nine times out of a hundred, the ghost is the victim, because the only thing tying them to this world is their grudge. That's why they make shitty houseguests and surprisingly adequate politicians. Every now and then that grudge is based on a simple misunderstanding and you can clear that up and they go away. But usually it's real fucked up shit. And if you feed that grudge, shit goes south, as you've just seen."

"Why didn't you tell me that before I went inside?"

Over the radio a woman's voice said, "Agent Glass with SHU to Fang 9-01. We're about a block away. Update on the situation before we stage?"

"01 to Glass. Objects being thrown from the victim's home, already experienced the initial vent just after leaving the building, but the rookie provided a lot of validation before I could intervene, so there could be another few vents left in her."

Something heavy clanked loudly against the side of the cruiser closest to the house. When Green flinched, Valance turned to him. "Don't worry," she said. "On the fuck-up scale, this rates pretty low. It won't affect your eval that much. Plus, I'm sure you'll be the spark that lights much bigger clusterfucks than this throughout your career. Besides, the old hags at SHU love an excuse for a clearing. Nobody will say this out loud, but if you don't occasionally escalate a haunting to give them something to do, they can be real mischievous cunts around the station, drugging the coffee pot with love potions and experimenting with new wards that don't always—or rather, don't usually—work. A bored hag is in nobody's best interest."

A windowless white van careened around the corner at the end of the block, heading straight for where they were staged on the street outside the Chang home. Green could still hear objects shattering inside the house, and he genuinely hoped that causing such destruction might help Mrs. Chang feel a little better, at least. She deserved that much.

"What happens when they clear her?" he asked, hoping it was something involving finding peace and comfort.

"How the hell should I know?" Valance replied. "I assume she completely ceases to exist. Maybe she gets trapped in a spirit cage somewhere to be experimented on for all eternity."

Green's mouth fell open. "Why would you say that?"

Valance shrugged. "Why not say it? Does it matter what I say?" She popped to standing and waved until she got Lawrence's attention, then she hitched her thumb over her shoulder and pointed to the oncoming van.

Officer Lawrence looked in his rearview mirror, jolted, then started the engine and quickly took off with Charlie in the backseat.

"Best to get the suspect off the premises before SHU arrives," Valance explained. "They don't take kindly to the folks who create the stubborn hauntings, and if you allow a suspect to sustain a curse while in your custody, you'll find yourself with a serious lawsuit on your hands."

The white van parked parallel to Valance's car, and Green assisted his FTO in setting up road blocks on either side of where they staged before meeting the Stubborn Hauntings Unit agents.

The three women who hobbled out of the van were not who Green had envisioned. They didn't even wear uniforms. Or at least, it wasn't the one he'd expected. Once they were out, their arms full of strange glass vials and strings of objects that appeared in various states of decay, he glimpsed the back of one of their long cloaks to see the words *Kilhaven SHU* written in reflective lettering.

As one with fiery red hair, which stuck out from underneath the hood of her cloak, began pacing the property line, pouring a salt perimeter around the home, the other two approached Green and Valance.

"Catch us up," said the shorter of the two. One of her eyes was brown, one blue, and both were focused squarely on Green's chin as she spoke, making him incredibly uncomfortable and generally curious about whether he had a bit of spinach from this afternoon's cold pizza on his face for hours now.

He casually scratched his chin as if thinking hard about what to say. Nope, nothing on his fingers. Maybe she was just a weirdo who didn't look people in the eyes.

Green then launched into Mrs. Chang's tale, which was news to Valance, as well, and by the end of it, all three women shook their heads disapprovingly. "Typical shifter," the taller of the two SHU agents said. As she shook her head, a strand of straight brown hair with gray flecks slipped out from her hood. She resembled a human of about sixty, and a fairly pretty one for her age, except for her teeth. She had way too many teeth, and Green tried not to stare at them as she spoke.

"Yeah," said the squat one, who Valance had introduced as Agent Glass, "she ain't getting over *that* anytime soon."

Officer Valance nodded, and then said to Green, "I ran

involvement on Charlie Chang before I met you inside, and nothing came up. Looks like her death wasn't reported, which means ..." She looked at the smaller officer, who seemed to be in charge.

"Which means we need a shovel if we're going to have any success here."

Valance nodded. "Let me see if Mrs. Chang has been reported missing, and then we'll need to track down Jennifer Macintyre and get a statement from her. It'll be nice to lock shifter trash like Charlie away for a long time. Almost makes this shitty job worth it." She sighed wearily. "Green, you stay here and help Agents Glass, Saffron, and Stonewall with whatever they need."

He nodded and once Valance was back in the car, he turned to the short one, Agent Glass. "Sorry I escalated things. This is my first vengeful spirit call."

Glass set the objects in her arms down onto the hood of the car and placed a comforting hand on his shoulder, the way his granny used to do before she passed a decade earlier.

"Don't worry about it, Rookie. It's easy to get sucked into the spirit's story. The fact that you fell so deeply into it just shows that you're a highly empathetic human. That's good for a police officer ... regardless of what Officer Valance says." She grinned, showing her teeth, and he was relieved that she had a generally acceptable number of them. "Don't let her fool you; there was a time not too long ago where she had a few drops of empathy in her, too."

"Who?" Green asked, genuinely unsure. The pronoun *her* implied Valance, but the context was all wrong.

"Officer Valance. She wasn't always such a frigid she-wolf."

With a last pat on his bicep, Agent Glass grabbed what looked remarkably like a decaying human foot out of the pile on the hood of the car, said, "Also this call might be a good lesson for you: if you screw over a woman, she *will* find a way to ruin your life." And then she shuffled past the salt perimeter to begin the clearing ritual.

CHAPTER TWELVE_

Week six was wearing on Green. He sighed and leaned back against the squad car, still grasping the mistress's cuffed wrists firmly, waiting for Valance to return from the house with word from Homicide.

His final week on field training was equal parts relief and anxiety. On the one hand, not having Valance hovering over him all the time would likely allow his professional skills a little more space to breathe. But on the other the thought of going solo, arriving first on a scene and having to wait for backup, overwhelmed his mind's fear receptors so that every time he tried to visualize it, he ended up thinking about something else—mostly Becky Hellstrom naked in his bed, all curves and warmth. Admittedly, that wasn't a terrible default.

He still had to pass his final evaluation, which meant answering to a board of superiors who would review his daily evals, ask him tactical and ethical questions, and then decide if the City of Kilhaven was willing to continue providing him weapons, authority, insurance, and—should the first two ever result in the worst-case scenario—legal counsel.

Valance had hinted throughout the evening that as long as he didn't shoot anyone in the next week, she might just give her seal of approval in his final evaluation. Her support weighed heavily in the decision since she knew his skills better than any of the others on the panel.

Don't shoot anyone and don't piss off Valance. You got this, Norman. Homestretch.

It was roughly four fifteen in the morning, the time when Green was either finding his second wind or discovering that there was no second wind to be had. Tonight, there was no second wind to be had.

Valance strutted out of the house and made her way down to Green. "Detectives have it from here."

"I can't believe he's dead," whimpered the mistress. "I was just there with him. He was alive just an hour ago."

"Yeah, well," Valance replied, sounding nearly as tired as Green felt, "that's the risk you run when you mix heroin and strenuous screwing." Valance opened the car door and Green helped the woman into the backseat.

"Wait," shouted Cathy the Mistress from the back, "you think our love-making caused his death?"

Valance leaned down from where she stood by the open back door, looking Cathy in the eyes and responding calmly. "No, ma'am, I didn't say that. I haven't decided what I think caused his death. I'm torn between the heroin and strangulation, honestly."

As Cathy began sobbing, even Green could tell they were crocodile tears, so he didn't mind when Valance slapped the top of the car and said, "Can it. Even if it were accidental, you shouldn't have been fucking him anyway. It's called karma."

She raises a solid point, Green thought. Cathy shouldn't have been messing around with the deceased, and it was hard to muster much sympathy for her when the deceased's wife was the actual victim here—even if she did whoop Cathy's ass in the muddy front yard when she'd discovered that not only was her husband dead from an overdose of an addiction she didn't know anything about, but his death was called in by a lover she didn't know existed.

Brooks put the wife into her cruiser and strolled over. "Ya kinda hate to make these arrests, don't ya?" she said to Valance.

"Your lady, yes. Mine, no. I didn't know it when I started, but I think arresting shit-for-brains bimbos who can't seem to keep from sticking things in their veins and snatches are exactly why I keep putting on this damn androgynous uniform day after day and cleaning up whatever unidentified bodily fluids the universe throws at me. It's worth it, knowing you're making a difference."

Brooks nodded along serenely. "I see why you'd feel that way, Valance, but damn, you're a bitch. Like, all the time. It'd be entertaining if it didn't wear at my last goddamn nerve."

Valance shrugged, and after casting a sympathetic look at Green, Brooks headed back to her car and drove away with the wife.

Valance and Green loaded up as well, with Green in the driver's seat, and made for the jail. On a Saturday night, the booking process would take a while, but that was fine; it meant this was probably the last call of the night. He could really use some sleep.

"I've never been in trouble with the law," said the mistress from the back seat.

"I can't stress enough how much I want you to shut the hell up," Valance replied, pressing her palms into her eye sockets.

"My boss is going to kill me. He has a zero-tolerance policy about being late to work. What am I going to do without my job?"

Valance twisted in her seat and banged on the plastic divider. "Neither Officer Green nor I give two steamy shits about your job, to be honest. Maybe you can go pro with the fucking other people's husbands thing. I hear that pays well. You might even make it a few years before being murdered by a john."

More on impulse than anything else, Green found himself inclined to intervene with Valance's harsh conversation. But, God help him, he was starting to enjoy it. Why do this job if you didn't get to revel in the times when justice could be served? Certainly *some* justice was going to be served to Cathy, but probably not enough in the end.

Green thought back to when they arrived on scene. At first, things were per usual with an overdose—girlfriend was panicked, a little in shock, vomit was pretty much everywhere in the bedroom with deceased, CPR was a flop. Things had gone south quickly once the wife arrived, though. Green couldn't fault her for dragging Cathy from the house by her weave and laying a serious smackdown on her. The only reason Green had bothered to stop it when no other officers seemed in a hurry to do so was because the wife appeared *incredibly* pregnant. Mostly because she was.

Add that to the list of reasons Green didn't mind Valance's harassment.

It probably also didn't hurt that he knew he wouldn't have to spend as much time with Valance starting the following workweek. Sure, they'd occasionally be on the same calls, but the long lectures in the car and nerve-wracking, unsympathetic behavior on scene wouldn't be a major part of his life.

And shit, did that actually make him a little sad? He certainly hadn't expected the thought to sting as it did.

Stockholm syndrome, that's all it is.

As Green pulled away from the curb, heading toward jail, Valance said, "I had a man cheat on me once." She sighed. "Key word being *once*."

God help any man who crossed Valance like that. The thought sent a shiver crawling down Green's spine, one so strong it almost outweighed the shocking revelation that Valance, at some vague point in time, had a lover. A male lover. "He must not have valued his life."

She shrugged a shoulder in vague agreement. "He didn't value his career, that's for sure."

"And what career was that?"

She glanced over at him quickly. "You haven't heard yet, then. Huh." She focused her attention back through the windshield. "He was a cop."

"Oh."

"Go ahead, Rookie."

"Go ahead with what?"

"Questions. You like asking stupid and personal questions, don't you?"

Oh sure, he had questions, but this felt like a straight-up trap. "No, your business is your business."

She nodded. "Right answer. Maybe I can relax next week

without constantly worrying that you'll get yourself shot on the easiest call."

He let a small grin slip through, and he looked over at his FTO. "You're worried about me?"

She pressed her lips together and shook her head. "Not so much. I'm worried about my *career*. Your untimely demise would, at the very least, mean a demotion from field training officer for me, and I don't want to lose that extra bit on my paycheck each month."

"Ah. Okay."

"But while we're on the subject of possibly losing one's job, you should reconsider the whole sticking your dick in Hellstrom thing."

Green sucked in air quickly, causing him to choke on his saliva. He coughed and gagged until he caught his breath again. "How long have you known?"

"Like I've been keeping track. How long have you been giving it to her hate-curdled lady parts?"

"They're not hate—"

She held up a hand to stop him. "Gross. I don't want to know the details. Just answer the question, then I'll answer yours."

He thought about it. "I guess about a month?"

"Then I've know about it for about a month. And I suspect anyone with a decent nose has known about it for that long, too. Your hygiene practices need work."

"I always shower after—"

"It's called exfoliation, Green. And anyway, it doesn't matter if you're banging her, at least not to me. I just want to go on record and say it's a terrible idea that could cost you your job, especially if any of the officers she's banging in other sectors find out."

"Other … what are you talking about?"

"I'm just being honest with you, Green. I think you're not entirely shitty at your job and you don't lack as many vertebrae as most of the people in this department; I'd hate to see you lose your job the same way my ex-husband lost his—over some dumb love triangle."

"You're just saying that about her having other men. You don't have any proof."

She set her jaw and nodded. "I understand why you wouldn't want to see it. I'd bet the signs were all there for the wife of that gooey OD-ed shifter back there, too, but she didn't choose to see it until it was shoved in her face in the form of this cheap pro-bono hooker." She jabbed a thumb toward the back seat.

Cathy shouted, "I ain't no pro-boner hooker!"

Valance rolled her eyes. "Remember that thing about the right to remain silent? It's legalese for shut the hell up."

"I don't even understand why you're taking me to jail. I didn't do nothin'! She attacked me! I'm the victim here."

"Green, would you like to explain the charges?"

Refocusing on something other than *oh my God, Valance knows about Hellstrom* was a struggle for Green's tired brain. But he had a job to do.

"Ma'am, you were found with a dead body that showed clear indicators of an overdose, and you've exhibited all the signs of being high on heroin yourself. In addition, there were signs of swelling in the deceased's face that suggest he was dead before the heroin was injected—strangled, if the marks on his neck are to be believed—and since you were the one with him when he died, you're being held on charges of murder."

"Murder! That sonofabitch did it to himself! He never knew when to say when."

"Just shut up," Valance said. "We know you did it. You strangled the bastard and then injected him to make it look like an accident. I get it, okay? Men are scum. He probably deserved it."

Cathy nodded. "He did."

"What, did he finally grow a conscience when he got tired of you and try to break things off? Did he find some new piece of ass that's just a little younger than you and who doesn't have the same cellulite on the back of her thighs when she wears some fetishy schoolgirl uniform?"

"No! I didn't kill him!" She squirmed uncomfortably in the back seat, and Green noted that the tears were gone.

"Then what was it?" Valance asked. "Listen, I get it. That man I mentioned who cheated on me? I didn't mention this before, but I eventually murdered him."

"Really?" both Cathy and Green asked. Valance shot Green a scornful look, then turned in her seat to face Cathy. "Yes. And when the jury heard my case, saw the way he did me wrong, they let me go. Cleared of all charges. And look at me now, I'm a goddamn cop!" She laughed lightheartedly, and Cathy even chuckled a little, relief cracking through slightly.

"If I just tell them why I did it, you think they'll let me off?"

"I dunno," Valance said. "Depends on why you did it."

Green could sense the giddiness coming off Valance in waves. It couldn't be this easy, could it? No one would be so stupid as to let a little bit of baiting result in a confession of—

"He said my asshole had gotten too loose."

Green accidentally tapped the brakes but regained muscle control quickly.

So it could be that easy. Thank goodness for dumb-as-rocks drug addicts, he supposed.

Valance nodded. "Yeah, I'd say that's a good enough reason. Typical men, just use a woman up then complain about how she's used up. That'd make me strangle someone to death too. I bet it felt good, didn't it?"

Cathy nodded. "Oh yeah."

Valance sighed and turned around to face the road again. "Well, I hope it felt good enough to spend your life in prison. Because that's where you're headed." She smacked Green's arm with the back of her hand. "A woman scorned, Green. Keep it in mind."

Oh, he would. The night had seared that lesson into his mind multiple times over. But he wasn't sure who the warning pertained to more: Hellstrom or Valance.

———

"Can I ask you something?" Green stared down into Becky's eyes where she lay naked beneath him early the next morning. Interrupting foreplay with conversation was not what he would normally consider a 'smart move,' but this was important. It'd been nagging at him for a solid day.

"Sure," she said sweetly. "Anything."

"Why did you give me the cold shoulder the other night when Valance and I brought in that murder suspect?"

She squinted up at him and blinked rapidly. Clearly, this wasn't the kind of question she'd expected. "I— What are you talking about?"

"The human woman who tried to stage her lover's

overdose. When we brought her in, you were there, and you didn't even smile at me." He rolled off her. Pinning her down underneath him while confronting her seemed just a little too intense, and the last thing his career needed was a domestic abuse charge.

She frowned. "I didn't realize I did that. I was just in a bad mood that night."

"You seemed to have plenty of smiles for Officer Stafford." He didn't mean to sound juvenile, but he couldn't contain it.

She rolled onto her side to face him, propping her head up on her elbow. "You sound jealous. I smile at one long-time friend and you get your hackles up?"

Human friend, he thought bitterly. "You practically ran off with him and his suspect when you saw me come in. You stuck me with Nurse Ulster, for christsake!"

"She's not so bad."

"Please. She's terrible. She conducts cavity searches the same way I dig a hair clot from my bathroom drain."

"You're overthinking it, Norman."

"No," he insisted, "she's *really* rough on those cavity searches. It's disturbing."

"Not that. The other night."

"Valance knows," he spat.

She nodded, understanding finally settling into her face, relaxing the lines at the corners of her eyes. "Ah, okay. And, yeah. Of course she knows."

"You knew she knew?"

She smiled pleasantly and tapped a finger to her head.

Green groaned. "Oh, right. Why didn't you tell me?"

"I didn't think Valance was a factor in our relationship, Norm."

"Obviously she's not. But you could've warned me. You know she hates you. I was totally blindsided when she called me out on it."

Becky sighed and adjusted to brace her head on her hand. "And when was this?"

"The other night."

"So, Valance brings up our relationship and you're suddenly jealous because I spoke with another male officer and didn't, what, suck your dick in public? I don't suppose Valance mentioned anything else about me, did she?"

Green struggled to rid his mind of the image Becky had no doubt unintentionally left him with at the mention of her sucking his dick in public. Finally, he said, "She doesn't think I'm the only one you're sleeping with." He stared into her eyes, looking for confirmation that the accusation had no validity. He couldn't conclusively find what he was looking for, even though he had no idea what it would look like.

But she shook her head slowly. "Norman, that's just ridiculous. I've spent almost every morning with you since we first got together. We've spent hours talking and ... I thought you would know by now what I feel for you."

"And what's that? What do you feel for me?"

She inched closer, pressing her full, naked body against him, leaving just a little space for her hand to slide between their bodies until her fingertips wrapped firmly around his base. "I love you, Norman. I'm in love with you."

Whoa. It seemed a little sudden if he was honest with himself. But women were *usually* the first to say that, weren't they? Then it was the man's job to lie until it stopped feeling wrong.

She started moving her hand along the length of him,

and despite only a month of whirlwind nights and early mornings feeling somewhat insubstantial grounds for love, he knew there was only one thing he could say to keep her touching him the way she was just then. And hey, he *loved* the way she got him off, so that was sort of like what she was talking about, right? Weren't there like fifty different kinds of love anyway?

"I love you too, Becky." Then he rolled onto his back, giving her an open invitation to show him just how much she loved him.

CHAPTER THIRTEEN_

Running lights and sirens, tearing down highways, weaving in and out of traffic, blowing through red lights—it was the ideal way to cap off the last night of his last week on FTO, and Green vowed that the moment these things stopped making his heart race, he would retire from the Force. He couldn't imagine that day ever coming, though. Even the fifteen-year veterans like Officer Harmon, who, for whatever godforsaken reason, had decided to stay on patrol, said this was the best part of the job, bar none. That wasn't to say the veterans didn't still find satisfaction in knowing they were helping keep the community safe. But driving fast? Driving fast was incredible. Maybe it was just the rush of doing something he'd been raised his whole life not to do, and not only doing it but being *ordered* to do it, commanded by urgency, implored by his valuation of the lives of others.

Yeah, there was nothing that could top the self-righteous rush of speeding without the fear of reprimand.

While ninety-five percent of his brain was absorbed in the thrill of running code clear across the sector, the remaining five percent was acutely aware of Valance's overwhelming displeasure at not being behind the wheel herself. He could feel the jealousy radiating off of her as they careened around a corner onto the frontage road, en route to Graveyard Shift bar, where a fight had reportedly broken out in the parking lot.

As was apparently the case whenever a situation escalated at the Graveyard Shift, multiple officers were assigned to the call. Dealing with that many drunk shifters —particularly the less than trustworthy type hanging around that place—was not a one- or two-person job. Not even a five-person job.

From what Green could tell, Officer Aliyah Brooks, Officer Tara Marrow, Officer Jeremy Lawrence, and Knox's replacement, Corporal Bruce Bannockburn, were all en route.

Maybe that would be enough.

Corporal Bannockburn pulled into the parking lot through a side entrance just as Green pulled in from the frontage road. A crowd of perhaps four dozen was gathered not far from the front doors, bodies moving restlessly around each other to get a better look toward the epicenter of excitement.

The car wasn't even in park before Valance jumped out and jogged over, shouting, "Kilhaven Police! Clear out!"

While she usually had a formidable voice, it fell flat underneath the sound of the crowd.

Corporal Bannockburn took a different, undeniably better approach, and by the time Green had moved the car out of the way of the entrance and headed over to the fray, Bannockburn was shouting through his bullhorn. "Police. Please disburse, or we'll be forced to employ pepper spray."

With a mob that size, even Green knew better than to get too close. He caught up to Valance, who stood at the ready a safe distance away until more backup could arrive. "What now?"

"We wait for the others to show up, try to move out some of the crowd, and hope nothing goes terribly wrong."

"Sounds like a good plan."

"It's really not."

Green jerked his head around to look at her. "What? Why not?"

"Because something always goes terribly wrong."

Two more cop cars arrived on scene, but Green didn't get a chance to see who was driving them before four shots rang out from the middle of the mob.

"Oh shit!" Green shouted, flinching.

"God dammit!" Bannockburn shouted through the bullhorn before he could jerk it away from his mouth.

The plus side was that the sudden gunfire was enough to instantly cause a third of the crowd to shift into various breeds of bird, and the flock launched up into the night sky and flew away, leaving fewer bodies to worry about.

The drawback was that there was now a gun in the equation, and with that many rounds going off, the odds were high that someone was suffering from a severe case of bullet holes.

There was a moment of stunned silence in the crowd once the birds flew the scene, but that silence was broken by a scream of agony. There was a genderless quality to agonizing screams. Green could never tell if the voice belonged to a man or woman, as if at that moment all of society's subliminal messages that train boys to practice speaking on a lower register and train girls to sound sweet and flowery are blown to shit, and what remains is an androgynous howling from deep in the lungs. *May it unite us all.*

The remaining shifters quickly came to their senses when Corporal took the opportunity to up his bullhorn efforts to convey that not only were the cops on scene, but also those cops were not super thrilled about anything taking place.

Green was glad he'd kept his distance as the shifters began to change into their preferred speedy animal and take off in all directions, deer and panthers and coyotes sprinting haphazardly away. Green flinched as one deer ran right into the road ahead of a car, but the driver was able to swerve at the last minute and avoid adding another complication to this already chaotic scene.

Amid the circle of discarded clothes remained about a half dozen people. One was hopping around, holding his leg and hollering in pain, and the other one—

"STOP! Police!" Valance shouted.

The other one shifted into a bobcat, and the gun he'd held at his side fell to the ground.

"Fang 9-01. ID on the suspect," Valance shouted into her radio. "Jorge Salazar. Most wanted number three, suspect in the murder of Henry Franco Morrison, AKA Ursa."

When Jorge made a dash for it, so did Valance.

Bannockburn dropped the bullhorn, as if to join the pursuit, but paused first.

"Fang 9-80 to 9-90," Bannockburn shouted to Sergeant Montoya via radio. "Scene at Graveyard Shift has escalated. Requesting approval for a Fang-wide shift for pursuit purposes."

A moment later Montoya replied. "Fang 9-90 to 9-80. Denied. Continue pursuit in human forms."

Bannockburn swore then tried something else. He spoke into the radio again, ditching call signs in his hurry. "Commander Ybarra. Scene has escalated at Graveyard Shift. Officers in pursuit of most wanted suspect Jorge Salazar but he's shifted. Permission for a Fang-wide shift for pursuit."

His request was met with silence. Then, "Permission granted, Bannockburn. All officers in Fang sector have temporary permission to shift until Jorge Salazar is apprehended."

"Hell yes!" Bannockburn shouted. He yanked his gloves from his belt and wrapped them around his silvers, which he stuck between his teeth. Then he stripped off his duty belt, followed by the rest of his clothes, and transformed rapidly into a timber wolf, cuffs clutched tightly in his fierce jaws, before sprinting after Valance.

Once the shock of the situation had dulled a little, it occurred to Green that there was a gun just sitting on the ground unattended, and he ran for it and scooped it up.

The man clutching his injured leg didn't seem to understand *what* Green was running toward, and his eyes widened and he shifted hurriedly into a brown bear and made for the side of the building.

"Feels like Christmas, y'all," Brooks said, then she performed the same trick with the cuffs as Bannockburn had. The academy definitely hadn't covered procedure in the case of a sector-wide shift permission. She shamelessly stripped off her clothes until she stood there in her full glory, then shifted into a black panther. Marrow followed her lead.

Watching the people he saw every day turn into animals

was obviously disturbing for Green, but Marrow's was by far the most unsettling of the group, as the woman who couldn't be above five-foot-two morphed into a massive black horse. The women then exited the scene, pursuing the wounded bear.

The four remaining witnesses to the fight also backed away, shifting into bears as well. Luckily for Green, they were much smaller than their wounded friend and had more interest in running from the police than mauling the lone officer who stood in the middle of them. Lawrence shifted into a coyote and hurried after them.

And suddenly Green stood alone in the parking lot, surrounded by a lot of discarded clothing and, once he focused on the piles of pants scattered around, more than a few guns and knives.

What in the hell was he supposed to do now? The majority of his shift was out doing the job, and he was stuck here with his useless human body. Running lights and sirens had seemed the pinnacle of police work, but by the looks on the faces of his fellow officers at the mention of a foot pursuit in shifted form, he guessed there was something even better, something he'd never get to experience. Maybe everyone *was* right about him being dead weight on the job.

Get it together. Find something to do.

But what? Where even to start?

His eyes landed on Bannockburn's discarded uniform and duty belt, still full of all his weaponry, and it occurred to Green that there were a bunch of Kilhaven police officers running around naked. Okay, he should probably secure the location by rounding up all the uniforms, maybe gathering some of the other discarded weapons, then whenever the rest of the shift was done having the time of their lives, he could help them cover up.

The weapons of the suspects and witnesses came first, and Green threw them into the back of his car as quickly as he could without sustaining any unnecessary injuries.

Then, with his arms full of uniforms and duty belts, he headed back to the cruiser and dumped the possessions in the passenger seat. "Fang 9-07 to command. We need a few more officers to secure the scene at Graveyard Shift. I have the rest of the clothing of the officers in pursuit and plan on returning it to them."

The voice that came through was unmistakably Commander Ybarra's. "Good thinking, 9-07. Glad to hear someone kept their head once I approved on-duty shifting. I'll connect you to dispatch to help track down the officers in pursuit and units will arrive on scene shortly."

"07 to Ybarra. Should I wait for them to arrive?"

"No, just go ahead, 07. We can't have a bunch of naked officers running around Fang sector. The elves will plaster that all over the news for weeks."

"Got it. Heading out now."

"Permission to run lights and sirens, Fang 9-07."

He started the car, feeling much less useless, and only a moment later the first location update appeared on the HAM.

This was it. Lights and sirens solo. The modesty of his naked shift mates depended on him. And probably the results of his evaluation depended on how he handled the night from here on out. *No pressure.*

He hit the voice command button on the screen, and each new update was read aloud to him over the blare of the siren as he took a quick turn left into a neighborhood, a sharp right into a more industrial road, and kept going, turn after turn, farther and farther. Had they really covered this much distance in their pursuit? It had to be miles already from where they started at the bar.

The first officers the telepaths led him to were Brooks and Marrow, who he found at the dead end of an alley between a lumber yard and a farm equipment depot. They held the gunshot victim between them, cuffs on his wrists as he moaned in agony. The two officers wore only gloves, which was slightly more than the victim had on.

Brooks approached the passenger side of the car before Green could get out, and she opened the door. "Thanks, Green." She smiled pleasantly at him, and he struggled to keep his eyes on her face rather than a little lower when she bent forward, rifled through the stack and pulled out two uniforms and the accompanying belts and boots. "For a second I was worried we'd have to hoof it back to the bar to get this. You're a life saver." She winked at him.

Marrow shoved the suspect into the back of Green's car and then the two women hurriedly dressed before Officers Harmon or Williamson, both notorious prudes, arrived on round-up duty. When his monitor started speaking to him again, Green followed its directions and took off to catch up with Valance and Bannockburn.

It occurred to him only as the automated voice told him he was just around the corner from where Valance and Bannockburn had managed to apprehend Salazar, that there was a good chance he was about to see his FTO buck naked. If his heart wasn't already pushing its limits from running lights and sirens the whole way over, the realization pushed it to a dangerous brink.

The automatic voice told him he had arrived at the

location of Valance and Bannockburn when he pulled into the parking lot of a small, forested public park, but he didn't see anyone.

"Where are they?" He squinted through the darkness but didn't see anything. He'd just have to go look for them.

He silenced the siren but kept the lights on as a beacon that might attract them to the car, then he grabbed their uniforms, crawled out, and flicked on his flashlight, scanning the area.

The beam hopped over a dilapidated jungle gym and a teeter-totter that looked more like a rusty launch pad than a toy for children, before a deep growl caught his attention not too far to the right of where he was looking.

He followed the sound, and when the ground sloped down quickly, he spotted two wolves surrounding the cuffed human form of Jorge Salazar. Salazar was sitting on the dry bed of rocks, acting like he wasn't flanked by two massive and snarling timber wolves.

Green stopping quickly in his tracks at the top of the incline, sending a small avalanche of pebbles sliding down the bank toward the others.

How in the hell …? Did they get those cuffs on him as wolves?

The larger of the wolves looked up at him first, but it was the smaller one that approached and shifted a few feet ahead of him. Bannockburn. The corporal nodded and took his clothes from Green. "Thanks. I apologize for the nudity." He slipped on his uniform and belt and then took Valance's from Green, bringing it back down the embankment and leaving it on a boulder a few yards away from where the wolf stood guard.

Green helped out by grabbing Salazar's wrists behind his back so Bannockburn could begin sending updates via radio while Valance moved over to the boulder, shifted and then began dressing.

She wasn't exactly hidden from sight down here in the dried creek with the moon so bright overhead, but it was clear the distance was intended for a little bit of privacy, which was why Green felt guilty when he finally caved and snuck a peek. But he was only human, right? And she was a woman, and he liked women. And he'd be a liar if he said he hadn't wondered if Valance could actually have a woman's body hidden under her obsessively starched and ironed uniform.

Turned out she did. Without the bulky belt, she had a nice waist and soft hips, at least from behind, which was the only angle he was granted as she slipped on her clothes. It occurred to him that she probably had breasts, too. He'd never noted them before, probably because she existed in his psyche as a sexless source of anxiety and sometimes even outright terror, but when he taxed his memory, he realized, yes, there was a little bit of a curve to her silhouette up top, even in a uniform. He couldn't confirm it in the creek bed, though, because she made a point of facing away from him. Like he couldn't be trusted to keep his eyes to himself.

"You slipping it to her?" Salazar asked, following Green's gaze.

"What? No. Shut up. She's my field training officer."

Jorge raised an eyebrow at that. "You're not a real cop?"

"Yes, I'm a real cop. I'm just finishing up my field tr—"

But he didn't get to finish the sentence before Salazar made a quick run for it, catching Green off-guard and slipping free of his grasp.

"Corporal!" Green shouted as Salazar headed straight for the werewolf.

Corporal Bannockburn turned, saw the suspect charging him and grinned before he drew his Taser and deployed it.

Even cool, calm, and collected Bannockburn cringed and then groaned when he realized one of the prongs had hooked into Salazar's sternum and the other had found the man's exposed scrotum.

Jorge Salazar crumbled into a heap at Bannockburn's feet.

"Goddamn," Valance said, finishing the last few buttons of her shirt as she approached. "What'd he do to you, Corporal?"

"Obviously that was unintentional, but you know what they say about karma. Total bitch." He helped Jorge off the ground then carefully plucked out the prongs from their unfortunate location.

Salazar squealed then began sobbing.

"Oof, yeah," Bannockburn said, grimacing at the bleeding puncture wound on Jorge's balls, "if I had to pick between a Taser to the scrotum and a crossbow to the face, I'm not sure which I'd choose."

Green watched a fresh drop of blood trickle down toward Salazar's taint. "Face. One hundred percent face."

———

On the drive back to the substation following the chase, Valance was more hyped up than Green had ever seen her. She could hardly sit still in the passenger's seat as she rehashed the call.

"That's the way every pursuit should be, Green. I'm

telling you. Before the lawsuits piled up too much for legal to handle, back before the damn elves over at the *Kilhaven Tribune* decided cops were enemy number one to their freedom, that's how it used to be done. Shift at officer discretion."

"Sounds fun." Green took his time getting back to the sub, dragging out the last night of his field training.

"And you did great, Green. You did exactly what I would've asked you to do. I mean, sure you let your guard down at the end there and Salazar got away from you for a second, but I don't think anything will come of it. Plus, it gave Corporal an opportunity to tase that shitlicker right in the frenulum. Maybe extra paperwork for the use of force, but it'll pay off for Bannockburn when he can say he apprehended Salazar. Frankly, it might be what saves him from a mean verbal spanking after going over Sergeant Montoya's head for permission to change on duty. Sarge isn't going to let that go anytime soon." But she didn't seem too concerned about it herself. Instead, she sounded downright giddy.

"You think he'll try to get Corporal Bannockburn fired like he did with Knox?"

Valance thought about it then shook her head. "First off, I don't think Montoya cared either way what happened to Knox. But also, no, I don't think he *could* get Bannockburn fired even if he tried."

"Why's that?"

She hesitated for a moment, but her excitement from the night loosened her lips. "The Bannockburns are an old family in Kilhaven. Before this place was overrun with shifters, it used to be firmly werewolf territory. The demographics may have changed over time, but people don't forget whose land this really is. Even the ghosts and vampires know better than to piss off the Bannockburn pack. Vampires might win out in the end, but the Bannockburns and their cousin packs would make it more trouble than it's worth."

"This is all common knowledge?"

"Somewhat. It's not usually said, so you have to pick up bits and pieces here and there. But that's not how I know about it."

"How do you know it?"

She chuckled. "Because one of the cousin packs happens to be made up entirely of Valances."

"Oh."

"You know, Green, I think there's a distinct chance you won't get yourself killed the first month out on your own."

He kept his eyes on the road. Seeing her naked was one thing, but receiving a compliment from her was more than his brain could handle right now. "You're just a saying that because you got to shift on duty and now you're in a good mood."

"Yeah, that's probably true."

As they turned into the vehicle depot at the substation, Green's phone rang, vibrating the door, where he kept it stashed in the side pocket. Considering the time of morning, there was only one person who it could be.

Becky.

"You gonna answer that?" Valance said, nodding toward the source of the buzz.

"Huh? Oh, no. It's probably just a sales call."

"Ah. I get it. It's Hellstrom, isn't it? You don't want to answer her call when I'm around."

"No!" he insisted, prowling the rows for a free parking

space, desperate to find one soon then jump out of the car to avoid continuing this conversation.

Valance chuckled. "Yes. That's exactly it. You don't want to talk to her when you've just seen me naked."

"I didn't look."

"We both know that's a lie. There." She motioned to an empty space and Green pulled in as his phone stopped buzzing. "It's nothing to be embarrassed about. I'm not convinced Bannockburn didn't ask for permission to shift on duty for the sole purpose of seeing me naked. Bastard's been stalking me for years. Point is, it's only natural for you to look." She reached for the handle to crawl out of the car but paused, turning back toward him and meeting his eyes. "Just make sure you don't moan my name next time you're blowing your load into sweet ol' Becky. I can't imagine she would be big on that." She moved to exit the car again, but paused once more. "Actually, if you *could* just moan my name next time you're giving it to that evil troll, that would be outstanding. Might make it worth the trouble of babysitting you for the past six weeks."

Green's phone buzzed again and Valance arched an eyebrow. "Whatever you're doing to her, you must be doing it half decently. Most booty calls aren't that persistent. Answer it." Once she opened the door and stepped out, Green snatched up his phone and hurriedly accepted the call. "Becky, you can't be booty calling me this close to the end of a shift! Valance—"

"Norman?" The woman's voice on the other end was not that of Becky Hellstrom. But it was familiar. Very familiar.

Blood shot upward from his crotch to his head, making him dizzy. "Mom?"

"Norman? Who's Becky? Norman?"

He had the impulse to shout "wrong number!" and then hang up and change his phone number to corroborate the story, but instead, he swallowed hard and decided to man up and own it. "Nobody, Mom. Just a dumb joke with the boys. Heh." Well, *sort of* own it. "What's up?"

During the short pause that followed, Green shut his eyes tight. At least he wouldn't have to face his mother anytime soon. Bowers was four hundred miles away, so by the time he next saw her in person, this whole, awkward conversation might be forgotten.

"Norman, your cousin Harris passed away last night."

Well, shit. Not to say it wasn't a long time coming ... or as long a time coming as it could be for a twenty-four-year-old fuckup. "How'd he do it?"

"How'd he— Norman!" But even Green could tell his mother's outrage was brittle in its foundation. "Your cousin is dead and you ask how he did it, like this was somehow his fault!"

"Tell me it wasn't and I'll apologize."

"It wasn't. Norman. Come on. This is family."

Green sighed and leaned back in his seat, his adrenaline from the night evaporating with each word his mother spoke. "Okay, fine. I'm sorry. How did it happen?"

"Some creaturist shifter up and shot him! Just like that! Your Aunt Rosie is devastated."

That was obviously not the full story, and Green suspected there was a lot being veiled to make Harris seem like the victim. "Sorry to hear that."

"The funeral will be on Saturday."

"This Saturday?"

"Yes, Norman. As in two days from today. It would mean

149

a lot if you could be here for it. You know how much Harris looked up to you."

Green tried not to roll his eyes. Harris only ever looked up to him when the kid was in deep shit and needed someone to bail him out—once literally. And Harris had never repaid a penny of that bail money he owed Green.

Guess I'm definitely not getting it back now.

He sighed. It didn't take a genius to know that funerals were never about the person who died; they were about the people left behind. Harris didn't—or rather couldn't—care one way or another about whether Norman drove his ass to Bowers for the service.

Exhaustion and anxiety swirled in his head at the thought of traveling home. His board evaluation was the following Wednesday, and he'd planned on using his three days off between workweeks to study until his brain turned to mush.

But there was no getting out of it, not at this point. Even if he refused, his mother would find a direct path to the guilt receptors of his brain, ensuring he couldn't focus on study materials for more than thirty seconds at a time. "Yeah, okay. I'll ask for Sunday off and take a long weekend. I can't promise they'll give it to me, though."

"That's fine, Norman. We'll have your room all set up for tomorrow."

"Tomorrow?" Sheesh. That could be three days in Bowers, which would be awful for two reasons. One, that was three days without having sex with Becky. And two, that was three days in Bowers. The closest thing Green had ever had to a sixth sense was the sensation of his hopes and dreams disintegrating the closer to that crap hole town he got. He suspected if someone blindfolded him and drove him out into the middle of the woods, he could eventually navigate his way to Bowers if he really tuned into his residual teenage depression; the stronger it got, the closer to home.

He'd heard about turtles and birds that migrated to their birthplace year after year, traversing thousands of miles and finding the same exact location every time. He wondered if maybe those turtles and birds had a sixth sense for hopelessness, too. Maybe they'd also been raised by a small-minded deeply creaturist family who blamed everyone but themselves for all their problems, and every year the youngest generation of turtles and birds had to complete an obligatory migration so that mama bird or mama turtle didn't track them down and guilt them into submission.

"Yes, tomorrow," his mother said curtly. "You haven't been home for almost a year and now you want to just drop in for a funeral and then scram? What, do you hate your family that much?"

He pinched the bridge of his nose. "No, Mom. I don't hate the family. Things are just busy here, and I'm just about to start—"

"Cheryl's sons didn't even have to be asked to come home. When they heard the news, they arranged for a flight right then and there. And they're coming all the way from Mount Pine. That's much farther than Kilhaven. Keller is already here—"

"Because he lives there."

"And you probably need a break from the city anyway. So many, you know, unsavory types."

"Unsavory types" was Megan Green's favorite euphemism for paranormals.

Green braced himself against what he said next. "Fine, Mom. I'll head home tomorrow."

"And? How long will you stay?"

"Until the funeral. But then I have to come back."

"Only until the funeral? Then I might just tell Aunt Rosie to push it back a week! Who knows the next time you'll grace us with your presence."

"Mom."

"What? Is it so wrong to want to see my son?"

A small tap on the window grabbed his attention. Valance stared back at him with a *hurry it up* look on her face. "I'll ask for an extra day off, but that's all I can afford to ask for right now. I haven't exactly had time to build up favors from people. I'm not even officially off field—"

"Fine, if that's all you can spare for the people who sacrificed the best years of their life to raise you, then I guess we'll just have to make do. I'll tell your father to start marinating some ribs."

"Okay. Gotta go, Mom. Just wrapped up a big pursuit and—"

"Fine, fine. I know you're way too busy to talk to me. That's alright, though. I'll have plenty of time with you this weekend. Love you, Norman."

"Bye, Mom."

"Aren't you going to tell me you—"

He hung up on her before she could finish and tossed the phone onto the empty passenger seat.

When he got out of the car, Valance was waiting by the trunk. "She dump you?"

"Huh?"

"It just seemed a little serious for a normal booty call.

Figured Hellstrom got bored of you and wanted to move on."

"No." Green breezed past her and opened the trunk, unloading his gear then the cache of weapons he'd collected from Graveyard Shift, setting it all on the ground by the rear tire. "It was my mom."

"Ah okay. Someone died."

Green paused. "Wait, what? How'd you know?"

"Has you mother ever called you at six thirty in the morning when someone wasn't dead?"

She had a point. "My cousin Harris. She swears it wasn't his fault, but I'm sure it was, somehow. She wants me to take a day off after the weekend and go home for the funeral."

Valance grabbed her bags off the ground and slammed the trunk with her elbow. "That's what vacation time is for."

He chuckled dryly. "Yeah, vacation. Not exactly what I would call it, though."

Vacations weren't supposed to end with the vacationer needing a goddamn vacation. But Green was sure that would be the case after a long weekend with the Green family.

CHAPTER FOURTEEN_

Norman Green stared down his dinner plate like it was a hostile transient with a gun. He was determined not to let the body-odor smell of his mother's brussels sprouts churn his stomach to the point of vomiting, but had this been a transient he was facing, he would have called for backup minutes ago.

It also didn't help that his stomach had remained in a tight knot for the past six hours. Not coincidentally, he'd crossed the city limits for Bowers six hours ago. Just in time to grab some fast-food for lunch and sit in the parking lot to eat in his car, buying himself another thirty minutes before he had to face his family.

But the inevitable had come, and it'd brought along with it the pungent scent of brussels sprouts. He'd never made it any secret how much he detested the veggie; he wondered if having these served to him with a side of martyrdom, due to his mother having "slaved away" in the kitchen to prepare a home-cooked meal for her children, was part of the penance she planned to inflict upon him throughout his stay.

His older brother, Keller, didn't seem to mind, but then again, Stockholm Syndrome had a way of erasing barriers and common sense and survival instinct. "Mmm, Mom. This meal is incredible. These potatoes are perfectly cooked, and the brussels aren't too salty."

Megan Green tucked a strand of her long blonde hair behind her ear and beamed at her eldest son. "Thank you, Keller. I'm glad *someone* here appreciates my effort."

Norman glanced across the table at his younger sister, Kim, a surprise baby who'd decided to drop into the Green family only nine years before, when Norman was already a sophomore in high school and well settled into his role as the youngest child. Not that he begrudged Kim for stealing that title from him. It was more that he felt incredibly sorry for her, but he moved out of the house before he could do much of anything to help.

Kim jabbed at the hemispheres of brussels, nudging them around her plate without putting them in her mouth. She propped her head up on her hand, her elbow resting beside her plate.

Keller was such a prick.

These brussels were like eating a raw dandelion, and the baked potatoes were so undercooked they were crunchy. Even a nine-year-old knew this food was god-awful and seasoned with spite.

Gregory Green stared down at his phone through the tiny reading glasses he kept on the end of his nose at all times. Norman could tell not a word of his mother's blanket guilting or Keller's ass kissing had made it through to his father's conscious mind.

Suddenly, though, Gregory looked up from his phone at his family, who he seemed half surprised to find himself amongst. "They say within the next ten years, Bowers County will be majority shifter!" he pronounced, outraged.

"*Who* says that, Dad?" Norman asked.

Gregory shook his phone at Norman. "They do, son! The real reporters! Not those damn elves who feed you all that horseshit up there in the cities. I mean real, salt-of-the-earth people."

"Humans," Norman said, trying not to let his annoyance show.

"Damn straight, humans."

Green wanted to point out that his father was doing to paranormals what he'd always complained about the white humans in town doing to him, a black human. But if Gregory hadn't gotten it the first dozen times Green mentioned the hypocrisy, there was no reason why he should expect it to produce results this time.

Megan laid an arm on her husband. "Now, honey, let's not swear at the table. I prepared this nice meal for the family, and I don't want it—"

Gregory shook his arm free of his wife's touch. "Better enjoy these brussels and potatoes while it lasts. Before long, we'll all be eating raw steaks because it'll be the only thing we can find to eat in the entire county!"

"Couldn't you just cook the steaks?" Norman suggested.

Gregory glared at his son. "That's not the point! The point is that the shifters are procreating like a bunch of rabbits—probably *as* rabbits, too, with the lack of decency those people show for humanity—and I don't know how I'm supposed to keep my family safe when we're surrounded by a bunch of unsavory types like that!"

Norman knew he should just drop it, but his mouth kept

going. "I guess the same way you keep them safe around all the current unsavory types in this crap-hole town."

"Norman!" Megan scolded. "This '*c-hole town*' made you into the man you are. If you're not happy with that, that's not the town's fault."

Her reasoning stopped Norman in his tracks while he tried to make sense of it. And that was just long enough for her to find her footing. "I didn't want to bring this up in front of Kim, but it's the truth, and she needs to know. Your cousin Harris was *murdered*. By a shifter."

Norman's eyes darted over to his sister. *Why would you mention that in front of a nine-year-old?*

But Kim's mouth hung open in a large grin, and her eyes were wide with excitement. "Harris was murdered?"

"Yes," her mother said emphatically, *"by a shifter."*

"Mom, that part doesn't matter," Norman said, groaning. "With Harris, it was a matter of spinning the wheel of creatures to see which one came up a murderer. Humans tried to put a bullet in Harris's ass—"

"Language!" Megan insisted.

"—put a bullet in Harris's *butt* like three times during high school alone. Eventually one of the murder attempts was going to work, and it just *happened* to be a shifter."

Gregory shook his head. "I knew this would happen. I knew you would go into Kilhaven, spend a little time with some of the urban dwellers and then turn into a spineless apologist for the paranormals."

"Norman was always the most sensitive," Keller added.

You're the thirty-two-year-old who's too scared to leave his mommy's watchful eye.

"You know I'm a cop, right?" Norman said, swallowing

down the spicy bile that worked its way up his esophagus. "My job is to arrest people for crimes. That includes paranormals. What's more, because I live in a place with a lot of paranormals, I arrest a lot of paranormals. Mostly paranormals, in fact. I'm not making an excuse for Harris's murderer, but shit, can't we all agree that fuck-up had it coming?"

Megan made her displeasure with Norman's language known by shutting her eyes, placing a hand over her heart, and inhaling deeply.

"Look," Gregory said, motioning at his wife. "You've upset your mother. But I guess that's what you wanted."

"That's not—" Norman bit his tongue. There was no winning. His only sympathizer—maybe—was Kim, and while the rest of his family wasn't afraid to use her for their purposes, he wasn't going to drag her into the fray.

"It's fine," Megan finally said. She took a quick sip from her iced tea and collected herself. "It's hard for a mother to see her son brainwashed, but I came to terms with the fact long ago that I couldn't protect you if you decided to move across the country and leave us."

"I'm … not … brainwashed," Norman forced out between gritted teeth.

"Of course you are, son!" Gregory proclaimed. "We all know you have to work twice as hard to prove yourself to those elitist paranormals. They think you're less than them, and they've trained you to believe it, too."

"No."

"Yes. That's the way it is. I've read about how they do that. Are you telling me that they view you as an equal? Are you telling me they don't resent you being a part of their world?"

"That's not … they don't say that."

"Ahh." Gregory waggled his finger at Norman. "But they don't have to, do they? They make it clear in other ways."

"They don't *have* to make it clear, Dad. It's clear enough every time I can't do something that they can. Have you ever thought about that? Have you ever thought that maybe we *are* less than them in a lot of ways? And maybe that's okay?" He slammed his fork onto the table; he wasn't going to eat this shit anyway. "I bet you've never thought of it in those terms, but you know it's true, don't you? That's why they scare you. Or maybe they just scare you because you've never bothered to learn about them. You know what?" He stood from the table and threw his cloth napkin into a pile over the disgusting sprouts, which was easily the most satisfied he'd felt since his mother had begun cooking dinner. "You haven't asked me a single thoughtful thing about my job since I've been here. You don't call to ask me how I'm doing. You just *tell* me how I'm doing. And I'm fucking done with that." He turned to Kim. "I love you, and I want you to be happy. I'm telling you now, our parents are fucking crazy and mean. Don't be like them. Resist them. Then move the hell out of this backwoods town as soon as you're old enough to board a bus to Kilhaven or literally any other town with a population greater than five hundred bigots and shrinking."

Kim nodded compliantly, her mouth a small O.

Megan rose from her seat too and slammed her hand down on the table. "You do *not* try to turn my only daughter against me."

"*Your* only daughter." He chuckled dryly. "Of course you think of her like that." He shook his head, looked around the table. Kim was staring at him with something

159

suspiciously like admiration, Gregory was red in the face, and Keller wore a smirk that Norman couldn't quite decipher but that bugged him all the same. He reached over and smacked his brother in the ear before heading out the door to get some decent fast-food.

CHAPTER FIFTEEN_

When he was growing up, the children in Norman's neighborhood told stories of witches who lived out in the rolling hills of the north and were able to harness the energy of the earth. They could cause it to swirl around them in tangible clouds until it condensed into a liquid they could add to their cauldrons for spells. He'd enjoyed that idea for some reason, and it had stuck with him, but he'd never believed it as truth.

However, when he entered the chapel for Harris's funeral two days after storming out of his parents' home and checking into a roadside motel, he was about ninety percent sure that his mother was able to harness the grief of the dank church sanctuary, causing it to swirl around her until it condensed into a liquid that stuck to Norman's skin, soaking in, mixing with his blood, and turning to a thick sludge of guilt and shame.

And all with a single look that seemed to say, "See what happened to Harris because you decided to leave Bowers?"

and, "There's something defective with you for wanting to leave Bowers and betray your own kind."

Taking a page out of Valance's dictionary, he thought, *Guilt is a real shriveled taint.*

He walked the long way around to the other side of the pews to enter from the outside rather than the center aisle. The detour was conspicuous, but it was worth it when he was able to slide in next to Kim rather than his mother, who was already crying for no apparent reason.

Except, perhaps, the funeral.

Maybe she was crying because of that.

It was difficult to buy, though, since no one really liked Harris. The most he contributed to the lives of those around him was good gossip and a catalyst for feeling morally superior. Perhaps that was why Megan Green was acting torn up; her quick fix for that high of self-righteousness was about to be lowered into the ground.

She's a resilient woman. She'll find another source.

Roughly ten minutes of people pretending to like Harris so they could have their thirty seconds of Bowers fame by speaking in front of a large crowd was about all Norman could take before he needed a little air. He made to leave, but as he tried to scoot down the wooden pew, he felt something snag his shirt and turned around to free himself, only to find it was Kim's hand that had caused the snag.

She stared up into his eyes. "Take me with you," she whispered.

He leaned close. "You don't even know where I'm going."

"I don't care." Her eyes were wide and watery.

He nodded, and she followed him as he moved out of the pew and toward the exit. He knew his mother and father were watching, and probably a few others, but he was fairly sure there was a proper level of decorum that would be observed about the speaker at the pulpit next to the closed casket being the only one who could cause a scene at any given moment. No one stopped Norman or Kim as they left the sanctuary.

Usually the tepid, humid air of Bowers County threatened to strangle him, but when compared to the church, it felt like breathing in crisp air rolling off of a glacier in the middle of a vast national park. Figuring it would be best to put a little distance between them and the church doors, Norman led Kim around to the side alleyway, where the garbage cans nestled between the red brick of the church and a tall chain-link fence covered in creeping ivy.

When they rounded the corner of the building, though, Norman found the space already occupied.

"Sammy," Norman said, pleasantly surprised. "Didn't figure you'd bother coming to Harris's funeral."

Sammy had always been a man's man—broad shoulders, robust beard, deep voice—and he was the only shifter Norman knew from his hometown who'd successfully managed to keep his species under wraps. "Didn't figure I would come to Harris's funeral either. But you know how mothers are."

"Don't I know it."

Sammy seemed to notice Kim for the first time. "Oh, hey there. Wait, are you Kim Green?"

She nodded and smiled.

Norman placed his hand on her shoulder, pulling her close to his side and grinning down proudly. "She couldn't take the bullshit either, I guess."

Sammy stroked his beard appraisingly and looked down at her. "Huh."

"What?" Kim asked.

He shook his head. "Nothing. Just a hunch." He turned to Norman. "You hear how it happened?" He nodded back at the church.

"Killed by a shifter is all I heard."

Inhaling deeply, Sammy nodded. "Yep. That's the short version. And the one told by the news, too. You're a cop now, right?"

"Yep."

"So you know."

"Know what?"

"That there's more to it."

Norman chuckled. "I figured so." Then, "Wait, do you know more? Do your people—?"

Sammy's attention flickered nervously to Kim and back. "First of all, no, my people don't all know each other. But yeah, I heard this through my people. And I happened to glimpse a copy of a sheriff's report that suddenly went missing about twenty-four hours after Harris's body was found in a shifter's home. Called in by the shifter."

"Why would the shifter call in the murder?"

Sammy cocked his head to the side and arched a brow at Norman. "I guess it'll be a while longer before you're a detective, huh? Well, that's probably good."

"I would call the cops about a dead man if it were self-defense." Both Norman's and Sammy's heads jerked down to look at Kim, who'd just spoken.

"Very good." Sammy sounded amused. "Maybe when you're older, you can move to Kilhaven and be an on-call consultant for Detective Green."

"That's it?" Norman asked, wanting to get back to the important issue, the one that didn't involve his little sister outsmarting him in his professional arena. "Harris was attacking the shifter?"

"The shifter says so. Said Harris was breaking into the the his home, so he changed into a mountain lion and defended his territory. The police report corroborated that before it went missing. Harris's gun was found by his body, there were clear signs of a forced entry, and they interviewed one of Harris's dumb friends who'd heard that the shifter was hiding a pile of gold in his mattress—information that he'd passed along to Harris the night before it all went down."

Norman allowed himself a few seconds to absorb the new reality. "Yeah, that makes more sense when it comes to Harris. But why are you telling me this? I may be a cop, but I'm not a cop here. I can't do anything."

Sammy waved that off. "No, I'm not telling you because I think you or anyone else can do anything about it at this point. Well, maybe the shifter's lawyer can do something about it, but probably not. My guess is the lawyer realizes they're sunk once he's sure he can't find the police report, and he makes sure that someone working at the jail who's a little hard pressed for cash forgets to put the shifter in silvers for a few hours and then suddenly—poof!—suspect has disappeared.

"No, I'm telling you because you've always struck me as someone who might be a little smarter than the rest of these small town bumpkins. After all, you got out as soon as you could and made for a big city. That tells me at the very least that you're not afraid of shifters. But also, I think it might be good for her to hear." He knelt down so he was on eye level with Kim. "There are always at least two sides to every story. Even if you only ever hear about one."

She nodded but didn't speak.

Sammy stood again, shifted his weight, and reached into his back pocket, where he pulled out a small pipe and a baggie of tobacco. "You mind?"

Norman shook his head. "News isn't reporting anything about a home invasion."

Sammy packed his tobacco into the pipe with a thick pinky. "Of course not. As much as I can't stand the shitty elven reporting, the human garbage that comes out of this town is even worse. Those bastards know where the conflict is found, and it's not in a druggie human breaking into someone's home on a bum tip and getting what he deserves. That might stay in people's minds for the duration of one commercial break as they get a little pop of endorphins from feeling superior to the lowlife. But a story about creaturist prejudice leading to a poor, defenseless human being shredded to shit because of his species, now there's something people can get behind! People on both sides will be outraged for at least the next three days. Humans feel under attack; shifters see even the most basic facts that the news is providing. They know themselves not to be the monsters humans see them as and conclude there must be more to the story that's being withheld." He puffed at his pipe to get it started, then through a lungful of smoke, asked, "You sticking around here much longer?"

"Nope. Heading out tomorrow morning."

Sammy exhaled. "Can I make a suggestion?"

Norman motioned for him to go ahead.

"Leave sooner. As soon as you can. There's a protest brewing for around four this afternoon on the town square.

Things might get ugly, but mostly I figure you don't want to be around when everyone's asked to pick a side."

"I'd say the same to you," Norman replied. "You're in a more precarious position than I am."

Sammy pouted out his lips and conceded with a slight jerk of his head. "Which is why I'm going back to Pan City just as soon as I finish this smoke and kiss my mother goodbye." He looked down at Kim again. "You don't have to pick a side on this yet, kid. And actually, I suggest you don't. If your mommy or daddy or Keller tries to make you go with them to the protest, just tell them your stomach hurts. Or whatever. Make up an excuse, okay?"

She nodded, and Sammy smiled sadly and inhaled deeply.

And as he did, his expression changed, his brows pinching together. His breathing turned to sharp, quick inhales, and Norman realized he must've picked up a scent.

"Damn. Elves. They're already gathering outside the church." He overturned his pipe, dumped the remaining tobacco onto the ground, and stomped out the embers. "That's my cue. Been nice chatting with you again, Norman. If you're ever in Pan City, give me a shout."

"Sure thing. Same to you if you ever come to Kilhaven."

Sammy scoffed. "Sure. But don't hold your breath. That place is a shitpit. So, maybe *do* hold your breath, or at least breathe through your mouth." He glanced down at Kim. "Well, uh, good luck. Nice to see you again." Then with a last apologetic look at Norman, he turned and headed the opposite way down the alley. Going the back way seemed like a good idea, but Kim needed to get back to their parents. He bent down to be on eye level. "Have you ever met an elf?"

"No."

"Me neither. I've heard they're annoying but not dangerous. I need you to head back to the church by yourself to find Mom and Dad. The elves might try to talk to you, but don't say anything, okay?"

"Okay. Where are you going?"

"Back to Kilhaven. If I go back over there—"

"I understand."

"Do you?" he asked, surprised.

"Yep. Adults aren't ignored like kids are."

He thought about that. "I guess not."

She hugged him and then casually strolled back toward the front of the church. He watched her go, then sucked in a chest full of air. The smell of the nearby garbage cans smacked his brain around a little. But there was also something comforting about that smell, something that felt like home. Not Bowers, because this wasn't home anymore, he realized.

Nope, his home was waiting for him back in Kilhaven.

CHAPTER SIXTEEN_

Sergeant Montoya flipped through the stack of daily evaluations on the conference table in front of him while Corporal Bannockburn, Officer Valance, and Lieutenant Fukumoto waited patiently for their chance to drill Green on his performance.

His early departure from Bowers had freed up an unexpected chunk of time to study for this evaluation. But no amount of studying could curb the sweat he felt soaking into the armpits of his dress uniform as he stood five feet away from the conference table, staring at the jury which held the fate of his career in its hands.

"I see your daily evaluations started off a little rocky," Montoya said, peering down through tiny spectacles that his large, hairy face swallowed up. Then he glanced up at Green. "That's to be expected." He dropped the paper back onto the table. "The important thing is that they improve over time, which yours do."

Green tried not to appear too shocked. But holy shit, Valance approved of him? His whole game plan for this interview was based around the presumed given that Valance would give him average marks at best and he'd have to talk his way out of it over the course of the half hour.

"How do you feel you've done, Green?" Montoya asked.

Green cued up his practiced response. "I've approached every day as an opportunity to grow and improve, and I feel I've done that. And I'll continue to do that on the job."

It had sounded much better when he'd said it into the full-length mirror at home, but now it just came out lame and boring.

Montoya seemed to agree, as he shrugged and turned to the lieutenant. "I'm sure you have some questions for him, sir."

Lieutenant Fukumoto nodded. Without glancing down at the legal pad in front of him, where he'd scribbled copious notes during the first fifteen minutes of the evaluation, he said, "I'd like you to run me through one of your calls. It took place in Shady Grove trailer park during your fifth week of FTO. You and Officer Valance arrived to find a deceased human and shifter, then I believe you called in former Corporal Knox."

Green's body stiffened as he tried to guess where Fukumoto was going with this. Foolishly he'd hoped that this case was in the past and would stay there, but maybe nothing in this line of work did that; maybe everything came back to bite one in one's ass. He wanted to look to Valance for a signal, but he thought better of it.

"Now, in the report that Knox filed," Fukumoto continued, "she indicates that the deaths seemed in line with a vampire murder."

Green held his breath but nodded slightly.

"Even though Knox filed the report, protocol dictates

you file a supplemental report since you and Valance were first on scene. But I don't see one of those here. Before we get into the why of that, I'd just like to know what you believe to be the cause of death of the two victims."

This time, Green did let his focus slip sideways to look at Valance. Fukumoto would likely notice, but it was better he have suspicions than Green flat-out make the wrong move here.

Valance shut her eyes softly, and her head moved side to side almost imperceptibly.

"I wouldn't have assumed it was a vampire, sir," Green replied.

"And what would you have assumed it was?"

Oh, God. He had to say it. He had to say this stupid bullshit. He swallowed against the humiliation. "I would have assumed it was a shapeshifter, sir."

Fukumoto tilted his head to the side and narrowed his eyes. "Explain how that would work, please."

Oh, for fuck's sake.

His eyes flickered to Valance again, and she nodded minutely.

"Well, sir, I suspect the shifter would first assume the form of a bear or some other animal with large claws, and take down the werewolf—a sneak attack, probably. Then the shifter would assume the form of an anaconda. Or a large, venomous snake of some other kind—I'm not very familiar with snake breeds—and then attack the human, perhaps constricting and then biting."

Wow, it sounded even dumber aloud than it did in his head.

But Fukumoto nodded. "Yes, that's what I suspect as well. One must always try to rule out the most obvious answer first, and the one you presented has a much higher likelihood than any vampire claims, which are, quite frankly, more conspiracy theory than police work."

When the lieutenant glanced down at his notes again, Green risked another peek at Valance, but now her face gave away nothing. Bannockburn and Montoya sat in the middle of the panel, Montoya pointedly avoiding eye contact with Green, Bannockburn looking bored and ready for this evaluation to be concluded.

Same, Green thought.

"Now that we've established you had a different point of view from Corporal Knox," Fukumoto continued, "I'm curious why you didn't fill out a supplemental report stating so."

"Well, sir, I, uh ..."

But Valance jumped in. "I'll stop you there, Officer Green. I take responsibility for this decision." She leaned forward slightly to see past Montoya and Bannockburn. "It was a special situation, as I knew that Knox would report it as a vampire killing when it obviously wasn't. Green was stuck between a rock and a hard place, having to decide whether he would directly contradict a supervisor or back up her statement when he believed it to be untrue based upon his experience. I made the call, saying it qualified as an exigent circumstance that allowed, as per department policy, for his supplemental report to be upon request only. I still stand by that."

Lieutenant Fukumoto nodded and looked at Green. "Did you ever receive a request from detectives to submit a supplemental report?"

"No, sir."

"Then I guess that case is settled. In the future, it would

be wise to submit the report, but considering your professional vulnerability during your probationary period, I do see Officer Valance's point about it being an exigent circumstance that would permit a report only upon demand." He glanced back down at his notepad. "Now, I see that on one occasion during your third week, you wrestled an alligator?" Fukumoto appeared pleased as he lifted his gaze from the table again. "Tell me more about that."

———

As soon as Green left the evaluation room and stepped into the hall, he kicked himself for not asking the obvious question: when would he be notified of their decision?

The door had just shut behind him, and he considered peeking his head back in before accepting that that was his dumbest idea of the day.

Luckily a couple of his buddies from the academy were sitting on a bench in the hall, waiting patiently for their evaluations, also in their dress uniforms.

"Green!" shouted Kilgore, an alarmingly tall shifter he'd studied with for their weekly quizzes. She stood shook his hand. "How'd you do?"

"Fine, I guess."

The other former classmate, Grover, stood too. "Heard you wrestled a gator shifter." He nodded his approval.

Green tried not to blush. "Yeah. Not one of my finest moments."

"Are you kidding me?" Kilgore said. "That's some renegade stuff right there. I didn't know you had it in you."

"I didn't know I had it in me, either. Hey, do you know

when we'll find out about …" He nodded back toward the room.

"I think it's a couple of weeks," Grover replied. "You worried about it?"

"Nah," Green lied.

While the rest of the evaluation had gone fairly smoothly and included ample praise from Bannockburn, Montoya, and even an unexpected endorsement from Valance, the issue of the supplemental report for the obvious vampire killing— and the strange unwillingness of Fukumoto to entertain that possibility—left Green with just the right amount of doubt to keep his heart racing and his armpits sweating. "Well, good luck." He shook their hands again and headed straight for the bathroom to splash a little water on his face.

No matter what happened, he could at least appreciate that it was over with. And it wasn't too painful.

As he left the men's bathroom, a familiar face greeted him by the water fountain.

"I have to say, Rookie," Valance began, "you managed not to screw the pooch completely. Congrats."

"Uh, thanks."

She took a step forward, leaving less than a foot between them. "You got your story straight, right?" she asked quietly.

He nodded. "Absolutely."

"Good. Because you looked like you weren't expecting it to come up, and you should have expected it to come up."

"I know. I should've guessed it would come back to bite me in the ass like—"

She chuckled dryly and stepped back. "Oh no, Rookie. *That* wasn't it biting you in the ass. But it will. It'll bite us both in the ass eventually. And when it does, you'll know."

Green wasn't sure what to say as Valance leaned down and sipped from the fountain. When she straightened up again, her mood had lightened. "Anyway, good work all around. You got it."

She patted him on the shoulder and then headed into the women's restroom, and he took that as a dismissal.

He inhaled, filling his chest with as much air as he could, then holding it for a second, trying to relax his shoulders. Then he exhaled in a whoosh.

It did nothing to calm him.

Only a couple more weeks of probation before he was, hopefully, officially a civil servant. Could he make it that long before the decisions he'd already made came back to sink their fangs into his career?

CHAPTER SEVENTEEN_

The shifter woman was leaning against her car when Green arrived on scene. She seemed fine, which was good, but he immediately wondered where the boyfriend, who'd reportedly been pistol whipped during the home invasion, was hiding.

"Mrs. Ramirez?" Green said as he approached.

"Miss. And just Jamie is fine."

"Officer Green with the Kilhaven Police." It still sounded weird. And approaching her alone felt even weirder. But it was just his first day flying solo; surely, it would get easier each time.

"Ma'am, would you prefer we stay out here or can we go inside?"

She hesitated. "Um ..." She glanced over her shoulder at the front door, running her left hand up and down her right bicep. "We can just stay out here."

"Is your boyfriend inside?"

"Yes, sir."

"Can he come out and talk?"

She hesitated again. "Yeah, but he's icing his head right now. One of the burglars hit him in the head with the gun, and he's got a big knot."

Green nodded, even though it was clear that was a bullshit reason not to walk outside. Something was up.

"Walk me through what happened."

As she retold the events, garbled to say the least, a suspicion grew in Green. "And you said you didn't recognize the intruders?"

She shook her head. "No, sir. I never seen either of them before."

"And your boyfriend didn't recognize them?"

She pressed her lips together tightly and shook her head.

"You sure? I'm not saying you're lying. I'm just wondering if maybe it could've been someone he ran into in public who heard about the cash or maybe a friend of a friend who gave him a ride home once and knew where he lived."

"I—I dunno, Officer. Maybe? But Caesar said he didn't know the guys."

Backup arrived, as was protocol, and Green glanced up to spot Officer Valance slamming the door to her car and sauntering over.

Green introduced the two women, and then said, "I'm going to need to speak with your boyfriend to get his statement. Is it okay if I go inside?"

It didn't matter either way; they'd end up inside eventually to inspect the scene and have her show them where the cash was stored before it was stolen. But it still seemed like a courtesy she deserved.

She paused but said, "Yeah, sure. Um ..." Green hitched an eyebrow, waiting for what would undoubtedly be a crucial bit of information. He was only on week seven post-graduation, but he already knew that "um" tended to be a precursor to intel that was necessary to survive the shift. So, too, were, "there's just one thing," and "I dunno if this matters, but ..."

"Yes?" Green asked, growing impatient.

She nibbled her bottom lip before continuing. "He's a ... were-coyote, I guess? And, um, when he was hit, he sort of shifted, and he's having a hard time shifting back." She looked like she was on the verge of tears.

"Yes, ma'am. Thanks for letting me know. I'll keep that in mind."

Green caught Valance's eyes, and she seemed to have the same suspicion as he did that something not entirely legal was going on that had little to do with the robbery.

The home was lit by a few dim bulbs behind the frosted glass of ceiling fans that hung dangerously low from ... seven-foot ceilings? Was it even legal to build a house with such low ceilings? Despite the fact that Green was just shy of six feet himself, he felt the strong need to crouch to avoid hitting his head as he announced his presence and then followed the sound of the reply to the dingy living room. The boyfriend, Caesar, was reclined on the couch, holding an icepack on his head with a small coyote paw.

As Green asked the man for his statement, he heard much the same garbled story as the one he'd heard from Jamie: they were sleeping, they heard the door burst open, a man they didn't recognize forced them out of the bedroom at gunpoint while another man ran into the bedroom and bagged the cash they kept under their mattress.

There didn't seem to be any outright lies, but there sure as shit were omissions. For one, how the hell did the intruders know there was cash under the mattress? Only someone who knew them could know that. Sure, it wasn't the most original place to hide valuables, but it was by no means a given that it would be there and nowhere else. It was clearly a targeted robbery.

While Caesar remained where he was on the couch while he recounted his story, his eyes darted from Green to the door to a few key places in the room where Green suspected he might find something especially illegal if he were to go digging.

But he wasn't in the mood to dig. There was enough surface-level shit in Fang sector to keep him busy without digging for more. As long as it stayed in people's homes, why should he bother with it?

"Okay, Caesar, I think I have it all unless there's anything else you want to add. Any guesses of where you might have possibly encountered the suspects before?"

Green gave Caesar plenty of space to respond, but the victim shook his head. "Can't think of a single one. I just go to work, come home, and that's my day."

More bullshit. No one did that.

Well, except for me.

Man, I need to get a life.

"And what's your last name, Caesar?"

The victim's body visibly tensed. "Why you need to know that? I don't have to identify in my own home."

Yeah, okay, this was something. "Well, sir, if you want me to file this report, I need your full name. Otherwise, it won't hold up."

Caesar's nostrils flared, and the creep of the coyote's body crawled up his arm, slowly fanning out farther from his changed paw. A clear fight or flight response, and one

179

most weres and shifters couldn't control without quite a bit of training.

Without even thinking about it, Green's right hand lowered toward his belt, his left hand still gripping the pad of paper and pen. "I should mention that providing a false name to a peace officer is a misdemeanor."

Caesar's jaw tensed, and the coyote traveled up to just below his shoulder, transforming a large tattoo of a desert landscape into a gray fur patch.

Then something seemed to soften or give out, and Caesar relaxed. "Johnson. Caesar Johnson."

Green nodded. "Okay. Is there anything you want to tell me before I run your name?"

Caesar nodded, looking like a small child confessing he took the last cookie. "I'm listed as a human."

If that was the worst of it, Green could handle it, no sweat. He radioed in the name to Valance, who ran it back at her car. He stuck in his earpiece so Caesar wouldn't hear the other side of the communication and was glad he'd done so when Valance responded with, "Son of a bitch is listed as human. Goddamn these undocumented weres. This could have been an easy call. These fuck-ups—" He pulled out his earpiece to focus on his immediate surroundings and decide what to do next.

Sure, he could take Caesar Johnson in for being an undocumented paranormal, but it just didn't feel right. Caesar was the victim. And there were all sorts of reasons why someone might not report their status that had nothing to do with being a fuck-up.

His mind traveled to Sammy, a man who was, by all standards, responsible but had a rock-solid reason not to report being a shifter: his family and his town would disown him. He'd chosen to live under the radar, knowing the possible consequences.

Perhaps as long as Caesar understood what it meant to live outside of the law in this one regard, Green could feel okay about letting it slide this time.

"You know, there's a good chance that whoever broke in knows you're undocumented and targeted you because they suspected you'd hesitate to report it to police."

Caesar nodded, appearing properly chastised. "You taking me in, then?" he asked. "Because if you're taking me in, please just don't cuff me in front of my girl. I'll just come with you. I don't want her to see me like that."

The tone of the request caused a pit to form in Green's stomach. There had to be another way to play this. Undocumented paranormals were up to officer discretion to handle since the first shift could come on later in life, and if there was no proof of a previous shift, there was no proof that the individual even knew he or she was a were-beast or shifter prior to the reported incident.

So, since there was nothing on Caesar's record to indicate that law enforcement had previous knowledge of his ability, this would likely be thrown out in court anyway, as Caesar could say he didn't know until this point that he was a were-coyote. Assuming he could afford a lawyer with half a brain who would advise him as such.

But it didn't ever have to go to court. Caesar was the victim, after all, even if it was clear he'd gone and done something stupid to call attention to stacks of cash in his mattress. As long as he didn't admit to knowledge of his creature status prior to the incident, there would be no need for silvers.

All that was left to do now was to convey that to Caesar.

But Green's recorder was still on, so he couldn't vocalize it. Pausing the recording would be suspect, and since Green had not yet received official word of passing his board evaluation, he didn't need IA on his ass right now.

Obviously, what he was about to do presented some ethical questions, but arresting a man who was a victim of a crime presented more urgent moral concerns, and Green felt fairly confident about the right answers to the moral deliberations.

He flipped to a new sheet of paper and wrote the words *yes* and *no* in big letters then held the pad up for Caesar to see.

Caesar's brows creased above his nose, then his eyes moved up to Green who asked, "Before tonight, did you know about your ability to shift into a coyote?" He tapped his pencil on the paper under *no* and shook his head.

It took a few seconds, but Caesar caught on. "No, sir. Tonight was the first time it ever happened."

Green nodded minutely. "And are you aware that you now have fourteen days to report yourself to the Bureau of Paranormal Affairs and declare your new status?"

He pointed to the *yes*.

"Yes, sir. I'll do that."

Green lowered the pad. "Okay, Mr. Johnson. Please do. If you don't and law enforcement has to come back out here for any reason, you'll spend the night in jail at the very least."

Caesar's mouth hung open slightly. "Yes, sir."

"I'm serious. Not only do you leave yourself open to being an easy victim when you live outside of the law, but you risk your girlfriend's safety, and I don't think you want that, now do you?"

Caesar shook his head, and Green tried to get a read on the man. He seemed appreciative, or at least like he didn't want this to happen again. Maybe he'd register. Or maybe he was just a lazy piece of dung and wouldn't even think about it for another five years until a cop showed up for some other dumb-ass self-inflicted robbery and saw Green's name on the previous report.

God, I hope this doesn't bite me in the ass.

But there was no question in Green's mind that this was the right thing to do, as a human, not necessarily as an officer.

Once the robbery detectives arrived, Green gently reminded Caesar to declare himself in the next two weeks then headed outside to meet Valance, catch her up to speed, and then write his report.

She glared at him as he made his way down the driveway. "Where's Caesar?"

"Inside with Robbery."

She cocked her head slightly to the side. "Aren't you forgetting something?"

After the momentary panic subsided and he remembered she was no longer his FTO, he composed himself and asked, "Like what?" as casually as he could.

"The suspect."

"Uh, the suspects are long gone."

She batted that idea away with a flick of her wrist. "No, the one inside. The undocumented were."

Jamie was only a few feet away, standing with one of the detectives, and Green could feel her eyes on him. He said as loudly as he could without it being completely obvious, "He says it was the first time he'd ever shifted. You know we can't take someone in on their first time. He has fourteen days to declare it to the Bureau of—"

"You know that's a bunch of steaming horseshit, Green."

As much as he wanted to back down from Valance's intense stare and mild snarl—maybe even find a nice hole to bunker down in for the next couple years until she forgot all about this—it was too late to go back. And what harm was there? It was a victimless crime, right?

"I don't know that, and neither do you. If you have some evidence to the contrary, you can arrest him and spend your whole night booking him in with your favorite jail nurse, knowing he's just going to be let off anyway when the court doesn't have substantial evidence to slap even a small fine on him."

As she narrowed her eyes at him, his lower intestines immediately alerted him that he needed to shit. And soon. Evacuate bowels, then run like the wind, his body said.

But he stood his ground, even as the little vein in Valance's forehead pulsed visibly in the low light of combined headlights pointing in opposite directions.

And oh, holy shit, were her blue eyes turning orange? Not good. Very not good.

She leaned close, speaking hardly above a whisper. "Put me on the record as saying you're an idiot for this, Green. And I say that as a shift mate who would hate to see you get fired and leave us down one until the city council gets its head out of its ass and ends the temporary hiring freeze. When he goes out and gets revenge on whoever did this—because you might be an idiot, but even you know Caesar knows the men who did this—it'll be your ass on the line for not taking him in and getting his prints on record."

She stayed close, inspecting his face, which he steadied against any signs of fear. Of course, his dilated pupils probably gave him away, and she could probably smell his adrenaline. But he wouldn't let it show where he could control it.

"If you know what's good for you, you'll go back in there and arrest him," she said. "Right now."

Showing any small sign of submission seemed far more dangerous than continuing. Green may not know much about Valance's personal life, but he knew she abhorred weakness. He wouldn't add fuel to her fire.

He doubled down. "Are you going to report me if I don't?" he asked. "Do we want to get started on that game?"

Run away! Quit the Force! Move across the country! Become a janitor! Just stop antagonizing her!

But he couldn't. It wasn't the right move here. It was like he'd suddenly grown a spine that he didn't particularly want.

Valance stared at him for a few moments more, then stepped back half a foot.

"No, that's not a game anyone wins."

"And you're not my FTO anymore, so you don't get to tell me what to do."

She rolled her eyes. "You're absolutely right. I'm not your FTO anymore, so when this comes back to bite you in the ass—because, in this line of work, no good deed goes unpunished, Green—it's all on you. Don't come crying to me."

Casting one last look at Jamie, Valance turned and stomped back to her car, and Green decided now was as good a time as any to inhale oxygen again.

He reached into his vest pocket, pulled out the notepad, and flipped to the yes/no page, staring down at it.

Then he tore it out, crumpled it up, and shoved it in his pants pocket.

A gentle hand on his arm caused him to turn around, and he saw Jamie staring up at him. "Officer Green?"

"Yes?"

She squinted like she might not continue, then she added, "Thank you. I'll make sure he goes to the Bureau."

"Then thank *you*." He nodded one last time and headed down to his car. Next stop: a quiet parking lot where he could type up the report and try not to think about how much shit he may have just stepped in with Officer Valance. Not only was she a formidable enemy he didn't want to make and someone with a say in the future of his career, but he couldn't help suspecting her desire for him to remain alive was necessarily for his continued survival on the job. And here he'd gone pissing her off.

He remembered Agent Glass from SHU's words about a woman scorned, and shivered.

If the time ever came when Green needed Valance to have his back, would she?

CHAPTER EIGHTEEN_

A frantic call for help that was cut short spurred lights and sirens on Green's vehicle as he hauled ass three exits down the highway, pulling into a quiet neighborhood lit in tiny showers of light from the tall street lamps. He bathed the dark crevices of the urban street in flashes of blue and red as he slowed to a crawl near the reported address.

Initial info from dispatch identified the suspect as possibly a were-beast or shifter, based on the ramblings of the woman on the phone. But when they'd run the address where the plea for help had originated, there were no registered paranormals located there. Just the presumably human caller and whoever was holding her hostage and had cut the phone call short.

Green was the first on scene, and he parked two houses down from the address, keeping his distance to avoid escalating this into some sort of urgent confrontation. He should wait until backup arrived, he knew that, but the call text had disturbed him for reasons he couldn't yet pinpoint, and it'd been minutes since the call had been cut off prematurely.

Phrases that used to mean one thing to Green held vastly different implications now that he was a cop. For instance, "I'll be there in a minute" used to mean he'd be there in a relatively insubstantial amount of time. But now, "I'll be there in a minute," could mean, "I'll clean up your fresh corpse." And "I'll be there in a few minutes," was basically the same as, "You're on your own, asshole."

He hoped he wasn't too late, though. Where was backup? Lawrence and Brooks said they were on their way, but he couldn't even hear their sirens. Valance hadn't responded to the call at all, and he suspected she was still pissed at him from their confrontation the day before.

Fuck this.

He crept toward the house, which seemed silent, the exposed and glowing bulb on the front porch like a nefarious lighthouse intended to guide sailors straight into a jagged, rocky death.

Going to the door alone would be a huge mistake. He could feel that in his sternum. But maybe he could get close enough to see something through one of the windows.

Just as he reached where the driveway fanned into the asphalt of the street, red and blue lights washed over the tree and mailbox in front of him, and he turned to see another police car park next to his then cut the lights.

Then over the radio: "Fang 9-02 to 9-07." Brooks. "What the actual shit you doing?"

"07 to 02. I just wanted to assess the situation."

"02 to 07. Well, ya look like a prowler." She got out of her car, closing the door quietly before jogging over.

"Lawrence is on his way, but some drunk transient flagged him down. He'll be here in a few minutes."

"So we're on our own."

"Yep." She drew her gun, aiming it at the ground as she crept toward the house. "That window," she said, hardly even a whisper. She jabbed a finger toward the pane just to the right of the front door.

The lights were off in the room itself, but light streamed in from a hallway. He silently made his way over and looked in to make a better assessment.

His heart dropped in his chest at what he saw, and he quickly dropped down below the window, his mind shouting at him that this situation he thought might be bad was way worse than he'd expected.

Officer Brooks tiptoed over and squatted next to him. "What is it?" She lifted her head just above the pane and then dropped down quickly. "Aw shit."

Green nodded as his mind tried to process the details. He'd gotten a clear view across the hall into a bedroom, the source of the light. The bottom half of a four-poster was visible, and that was enough to see a woman bound to the bed, her legs severely injured, if the copious flowing blood was any indication.

Green poked his head up again—partly to monitor the situation, but mostly because he was already starting to doubt what he'd seen. A shadow moved across the wall behind the bed then a man came into view, a large bread knife in his hand, and Green's stomach churned as he watched the man take a chunk out of the woman's calf and then move the piece toward his mouth.

Green dropped down again. "Oh fuck, he's eating her."

Brooks's eyes popped open. "What?! Who's eating her?"

189

"A man in there. He just—trust me. He's eating little bits of her."

"Fuck this." Brooks got to her feet, still crouched low, and sprinted back toward the vehicles.

She was just leaving him here? What about the woman? Shouldn't they go in and rescue her?

He followed her back to the cars, because *fuuuck being near that house alone.* Once it felt a safe enough distance from the house to speak, he did. "What the hell?"

She ignored him, instead radioing to Corporal Bannockburn. "… Yeah, Fang 9-07 says he saw the man eat a piece of her."

There was a pause once the corporal was caught up. Then Sergeant Montoya piped in. "Time is of the essence. Shift and get in there, Brooks."

"Sir?" But she didn't have to voice the obvious concerns because corporal did that.

"And leave all her weapons behind? With all due respect, sir, I don't know if adding *another* naked woman to this situation is the most obvious solution. If this man has his back against the wall, there's a good chance he'll kill the hostage."

"For all we know, she could already be dead," Sergeant said. "What would you suggest, Corporal, since you seem to know better than your commanding officer."

Was this clashing of egos entirely necessary when the clock was ticking for the hostage? Green's heart tapped out the unknown seconds until it was too late, and his growing panic only increased when Corporal Bannockburn said, "You know what we should do, Sergeant Montoya. Send in the Telekinetics Unit."

Brooks whipped around to face Green, and he was

comforted slightly to see that he wasn't the only one horrified by the suggestion. Of course, the validation that it was something to be horrified about eventually dawned on him, and the slight comfort was blown to shit.

Then something changed in Brooks's face, and she set her jaw and nodded. "I think that would be best, sir," she said.

"It's never best!" Sergeant Montoya raged. "The media already has us by our balls after the shift-on-duty call! Bringing in those psychos in TU will only make things worse. I guarantee it."

Another car rounded the corner of the street and came to a stop behind Brooks's vehicle.

Green squinted through the headlights, and guessing solely by the pronounced jaw, he guessed it was Lawrence.

Then the door opened.

Nope. Corporal Bannockburn. "TU is already on their way," he said to Brooks and Green as he strode up to meet them. "Montoya can eat my lupine ass. I'm not risking your lives when TU can clean this up in a heartbeat." He sighed and hitched up his belt. "Let's just hope they get here soon." He nodded at Green. "In situations like these, every minute counts."

It was nice to know someone else felt that way.

An armored Humvee pulled onto the street, coming from the opposite direction.

"That was quick," Brooks said.

Bannockburn shrugged. "Well, for the sake of transparency, on a hunch—and I usually have good hunches —I called them in the moment dispatch told me about the situation. But don't tell Montoya about that. If the sarge had his way, KPD would never use TU. But that's not the right way to think about it. Is TU full of fucking lunatics that could kill us all? Sure. But you gotta let the dog outta the kennel every so often, or it'll turn on you the first chance it gets." He nodded to the driver of the vehicle, then took a cautious step back. "You ever been on a call with the telekinetics, Rookie?"

"No, sir."

"Okay. Then I'll walk you through it. At this point, you're going to want to put on your riot gear."

"Huh?"

"Riot gear, Officer. And probably your heavier vest. All body protection you have, you're going to want to put it on. If you have a condom handy, probably wouldn't hurt to slip on one of those, too. Seriously, anything you got."

When Bannockburn backtracked to his vehicle, not taking his eyes off the TU van, whose doors were still shut tight, Green figured that was probably a sign the corporal wasn't pulling one over on him.

He turned to check with Brooks just in case, but she was already gone from his side, scrambling to wriggle into her heavy vest before lifting her riot helmet out of the trunk of her car.

Two other cars with *Telekinetics Unit* written on the side had pulled up beside the van, and officers jumped out and began knocking on the doors of the neighboring houses, evacuating the area before letting the TU psychopaths out of their cage.

The precautions were necessary, of course, if his lessons from the academy were accurate, but he couldn't help feeling like every second that slipped away only left the poor woman inside with exponentially more trauma, assuming she wasn't dead by the time the telekinetics were set free from their iron-lined van.

Finally, once the neighborhood was cleared three houses in both directions, the TU handler opened the van door remotely from where she stood twenty yards back, then dodged behind the temporary barricade she'd constructed.

Green stepped just a little farther behind the corporal's vehicle, positioning himself between Brooks and Bannockburn, because screw dying tonight.

A voice came through Bannockburn's radio, asking for a description of the situation. Bannockburn handed over the radio to Green. "Describe what you saw. In detail."

"Who's on the other line?" Green whispered.

"Detective Cummings. One of the telekinetics."

Oh shit.

"It's a secure channel," Bannockburn continued, "so don't hold back."

Green stared over at the van, from which not a single person had yet exited besides the handler who'd fled the front seat at soon as the van was in park. The sliding door was open, but from where Green stood, almost head on with the front of the van, he couldn't see anything inside the door, just a sliver of darkness.

"Fang 9-07 here."

A deep scratchy voice with a thick drawl slowly replied, "Tell me what you've seen."

The impulse to drop the radio and walk off scene, heading straight to the nearest temp agency was strong. Though Green had never realized it before, he suddenly became aware that he'd always imagined the devil would have a voice that sounded much like Detective Cummings's.

Time was of the essence, though, and the thought of the woman inside being eaten piece by piece was somehow enough to keep Green tethered to his spot. He inhaled deeply then began describing what he'd seen, including in-depth spatial descriptions, as the academy had stressed in communications with telekinetics. Once he'd said all he could remember that seemed relevant, he was met with literal radio silence.

Then finally Cummings spoke again. "You say he was eating her?"

"Yes sir."

"Good. Fang 9-07 you said it was?"

"Yes sir."

"And what's your name, Fang 9-07?"

Green's eyes darted to Corporal Bannockburn, who nodded him on. Sure, it was a secure channel, but there was an awful lot of survival instinct telling Green not to divulge his name to anyone on TU.

But at the same time, denying a request to a TU officer could yield quicker and more gruesome consequences.

"Officer Norman Green, sir."

"Officer Norman Green?" Cummings repeated.

Hearing his name repeated back to him in the voice of the devil made him want to head straight to the courthouse and change it, but he fought that impulse, along with the one that would've had him say, "No sir. Valance. Officer Heather Valance." But no, he didn't need to add arguments to her case against him. Instead, he confirmed. "Yes, sir."

"I owe you one, Officer Green. Taking out a cannibal is my wet dream."

Nothing else came over the radio after that, or maybe something did, but Green's attention shifted completely from his hearing to his vision.

Because two shapes emerged from the TU van, taking their sweet time as they moved across the street and stepped into the light cascading from the tall streetlamp at the edge of the driveway. Only then could Green view the two tall silhouettes enough to distinguish their actual attire —the long dusters, the gleam of freshly polished alligator-skin boots, the brims of two officers' black cowboy hats.

One with dark brown skin only visible at the wrists between his sleeves and gloves and on his expressionless face stepped forward and lifted his hands, palms out, toward the house. He leaned his head back slightly, so the light from above allowed Green to see that his eyes were closed. He struck Green as the ranking officer of the two, but who the hell knew why.

"That's Detective Lamont," Brooks whispered breathlessly.

The lighter skinned officer, who Green presumed through process of elimination to be Detective Cummings, stared down the house like it'd insulted his mama, and not a single thing in the entire block seemed to move. Could telekinetics also freeze their surroundings just like they could move them? This seemed evidence for it.

But then, when Detective Lamont swept one of his arms up into the air, a lot of things happened at once, all of which made Green especially thankful that he'd suited up the way he had.

The first thing that Green became aware of was the roof. It lifted. It rather, it *was* lifted, and in its entirety, sending large nails shooting off in all directions, clanking against windows and car doors and neighboring trees.

Later on, whenever Green thought back to that moment, though, he couldn't be sure which had happened first: the roof lifting or every single window in the house shattering, sending sharp glass shards out onto the lawn. Or perhaps the two events were simultaneous.

A three-inch glass shard hit the face mask of Green's riot helmet with such force that his head snapped back. He recovered just in time to see a figure emerge from the top of the house, hovering just underneath the roof, which levitated ten feet above the top of the frame.

The victim.

Was she alive or dead? Green was tempted to lift his face mask to see but knew better.

One of the ropes that had bound her to the bed still draped loosely over her torso, but otherwise, TU must have managed to free her.

She floated downward toward a pile of blankets set out near the TU van, and as she drew lower to the ground, Green noted a puddle of blood that floated just below her legs, trickling from her many wounds and settling in the air just below her, as if collected in an invisible bowl.

Her descent mimicked Detective Lamont's left arm, which he lowered slowly toward the ground while his right remained aimed at the hovering roof.

The sound of a rifle's rapport caused Green to jump, but neither of the telekinetic reaction in any way akin to fear. Detective Cummings flicked his wrist, sending a bullet skittering across the driveway, coming to a stop a few feet to the left of his boots.

Then Cummings looked back over his shoulder at his fear-wracked audience and spoke calmly in his deep crackling voice, "Y'all saw that, right? He shot at me." But despite the serenity of his tone, there was a look on his face that Green knew he'd be seeing again in many nightmares to come, a frenzied passion for destruction that would be quenched or else.

Cummings cackled maniacally, turning back toward the home and shouting, "Try it again. I just got lucky!"

Perhaps out of desperation, the suspect *did* fire off another couple rounds, but two more flicks of his wrists, and then Cummings and Lamont had nothing to worry about.

Then he waved his right hand casually, like he was motioning for someone to come closer.

And someone did come closer.

The suspect flew headfirst through the blown-out window, screaming like he was being tortured, but whatever agony he was experiencing didn't last long. Cummings brought the man all the way across the yard to halt mid-air just a few yards shy of where he'd planted in the driveway.

The suspect's screams ended so abruptly Green wondered if these telekinetics were skilled enough to control vocal cords or even sound waves. The entire street was so deathly silent that Green was able to hear the words Detective Cummings whispered to the man, crystal clear even across the safe distance of the established perimeter: "You shouldn't eat people."

The silence was shattered by the suspect's final agonizing scream as his clothes exploded off him in every direction, leaving him naked and exposed, and perhaps humiliated. However, it was doubtful he even had time to be humiliated before his skin peeled off him in a way that reminded Green of how he'd once seen a bartender zest a lemon in a single spiral that left the lemon completely bare by the end of it.

The flaps of skin flopped onto the ground beneath him

just before he exploded like a vacuum-sealed bag of chunky tomato sauce, painting everything within twenty feet in red spattering and flecks of bone fragments.

Cummings and Lamont were mostly left unscathed by the gore, but perhaps Cummings had let go of his focus just the tiniest bit, because he raised his hand up to his mouth, wiped two fingers across his cheek, lifting them to inspect the tiny bit of blood that had made it through his protective bubble.

He sucked it off the tips of his fingers, then reached into his duster and pulled out a radio. "Is the woman alive?"

The shaky voice of a medic replied, "Yes, Detective Cummings."

He nodded silently and then tapped Officer Lamont on the shoulder. Lamont lowered the roof back onto the frame of the house, then slowly opened his eyes, and the two TU officers turned and headed back into the van, closing the door behind them.

Was that it? Was it done? Should he applaud? Probably not, but maybe …

"Ho-ly shit," Brooks said from beside him. "I always think *this* time I won't need twelve weeks of therapy, but nah. TU calls always end with therapy." She sighed. "I'm gonna go set up an appointment." She headed back to her car.

Bannockburn cleared his throat and pulled off his riot helmet. "Typical TU show. Exceptionally efficient, so you're thinking, 'why don't we use these guys all the time?' then you're quickly reminded why you don't use those guys all the time."

With great effort, Green peeled his eyes off the gory blood-spattered front yard to take in the rest of the scene.

Officers and EMTs moved around with a terrified lethargy of those who'd just woken from a nightmare as they set out to tend to the victim, bag evidence and otherwise get this freak show on the road.

It had been a night of firsts for Green, and that trend wasn't yet over.

It was the *sound* of the elves that caught his attention first, the *ding ding* of their bells to alert anyone in the path of their fixie bikes move to the side.

They were not what he'd expected, but also somehow exactly what he'd expected. The look of them—their tall, lithe bodies, their attire of plaid and argyle button-down shirts, tight pants that seemed the worst possible choice for bike riding, and their fabric shoes—fit with the photos he'd seen before.

The smug sense of superiority was something he hadn't expected. Though maybe he should have, based solely on appearance.

"Uh, ex*cuse* us," one elf said when a TU wrangler didn't step to the side and the leader of the bike pack had to divert his trajectory to keep from running the woman over. He held up a laminated tag dangling from a lanyard around his neck. "Um, press have a right to be here." If a voice could sparkle, his did. Something about it reminded Green of a magic show in Bowers—a human magic show, that is— where the magician created a flash of light that was blinding then instantly nothing. Keller, being his usual prick self, had immediately explained it was called flash paper and added that the magician was dumb and either a fraud or a witch, either way being a sore the town needed to drain.

Regardless, the elves had flash paper voices.

"At least they missed the worst of it," Brooks said,

appearing by Green's side once again. "They'll spread the pictures of the scene all over the paper, but at least they weren't here to witness the goring."

"I kind of wish *I* wasn't here for the goring," Green said.

"Oh for sure. Same."

The TU van pulled away, but not before the small band of elves snapped their fair share of photos of the side of it.

The rest of the officers just ignored the elves, but it was clear the presence of them put a damper on already muted spirits.

"They need a couple of cops to wait at the hospital with the victim," Bannockburn said. "Green, since you were named over the radio, which these elven dickheads were undoubtedly listening to, despite it being a secure line, it might be best if you skedaddle. Brooks, you want to go with him? Give you a quiet moment to type up the report and, I don't know, cry or vomit or whatever you need to do post TU?"

Green and Brooks nodded, and Bannockburn headed over to where the ambulance had finally parked, now that the coast was clear.

"What'd you think?" Brooks asked as she opened her car door. "Best night so far or best night ever?"

Green exhaled in a whoosh. "I hope I never have to see those psychopaths again." Had he ever meant something so completely?

"You sure? Cummings said he owed you a favor."

A chill ran down Green's spine. "Uh, yeah. Talk about a favor you never want to cash in." He shook his head to clear the foreboding in his mind then packed into his car to follow the ambulance over to the hospital, where he would undoubtedly discover if he was a post-TU crier or vomiter.

His stomach was leaning toward the latter.

————

"I'm so goddamn mad I missed it." Officer Lawrence shoveled runny egg yoke into his mouth with a crispy piece of bacon. "I knew it would be good by the way the dispatcher described it, but that idiot transient decided that today had to be the *goddamn* day that he outed his buddy's meth house. I mean, talk about a boring call. I spent the rest of the night on inventory duty, carting out boxes of cleaning supplies as evidence."

"Well, ya missed one helluva show," Officer Brooks said.

She almost looked as tired as Green felt after a night of cannibalism and hospital duty. Depending on whether she'd opted for a good cry or for emptying the contents of her stomach, like he had, she might also be as hungry.

He guessed it was the shared experience of recent trauma that landed him an invite to breakfast at the all-night diner with Brooks, Lawrence, and Marrow, and for that, it was almost worth hearing his name spoken by the devil incarnate and seeing a man's skin stripped off him.

He looked down at the bacon on his plate, considered it, then went for it anyway.

Tara Marrow leaned forward conspiratorially. "And you said Bannockburn called in TU before even arriving on scene?"

Brooks and Green nodded, and Marrow continued with, "I don't know what to make of that guy." She frowned and sipped her coffee. "On the one hand, he seems to be no bullshit, but on the other hand, how the hell did he make corporal without being fired? Man never listens to anyone."

Lawrence chuckled. "How do you think? The last name says it all." He shrugged. "We're lucky to have him. Knox was good, but she was by the books."

Brooks rolled her eyes. "You say that like it's a bad thing. There are books for a reason." Then she grumbled, "Not like anyone in this fucking department follows them."

"Valance doesn't seem to like him that much." Green was halfway through the sentence when he wondered why he'd mentioned Valance at all. Too late by that point, though.

Balking, Lawrence said, "Of course she doesn't like him that much. She doesn't like anyone that much."

"She likes me," Brooks said.

"Of course she does," Marrow said. "You're hot."

That piqued Green's interest. But he kept his eyes focused squarely on his rubbery pancakes, while his brain mined for clues on this particular topic.

"Corporal ain't too bad himself," Brooks replied. "And as we just established ..."

"Wait, but aren't they cousins?" Green asked. "She wouldn't have the hots for her cousin, right?"

Lawrence arched an eyebrow at Green. "Distant cousins in the way all the timberweres are cousins, but hold the press there, because it sounds like Green is a little jealous."

Marrow punched Lawrence on the shoulder. "Stop being a dick. Green is too smart to go for someone like her." She turned to Green. "You know she got her ex-husband fired, right?"

Green nodded. "I did know that. And don't worry, she currently hates my guts, and she's not my type."

Brooks interjected with, "I'm near about eighty percent sure your dick disqualifies you from being her type."

Struggling not to appear *too* curious, Green asked, "Yeah, about that. Is she ...?" He didn't have to finish. The other three officers offered varying levels of certainty in their shrugs.

"No idea," Lawrence added to his. "Some things are better left unexplored, Valance's sexuality is *quite* high up on that list. She strikes me as a woman who might kill her lover directly after sex." Clearly, this was a tired topic for everyone else, and Lawrence redirected the conversation to a fresher focus. "Okay, Green. Tell me one more time. You saw him take a chunk off the woman's leg and then *eat* it?"

For a moment, Green became aware of how strange a mealtime conversation this was, but quickly his mind decided on two things: first, he didn't mind it at all, and second, he couldn't imagine having any other conversation after the night he'd had.

He bit off a hunk of a sausage patty and started in on the story again from the top.

CHAPTER NINETEEN_

Green's first week going solo had flown by, and his second week was going much the same. He wouldn't go as far as to say that he was getting the hang of the job, more like he didn't naturally assume he was going to be killed each time he was first on scene.

As the waxing gibbous moon crept toward full night after night, the action in Fang sector slowly heated up, each call making a little less sense than the last. That was fine, though, because it distracted Green from the main concerns keeping him awake each day between shifts: the fact that he still hadn't gotten official word of whether he'd passed his board evaluation, and Valance's respectably maintained grudge against him for standing up to her about the undocumented shifter.

She'd managed most impressively to never be on scene the same time as him, waiting until he assigned to a call before assigning herself to another call on the opposite side of the sector. Surely others had noticed by now, but there was nothing he could do about it other than hope it didn't affect his employment.

The full moon had already passed its zenith and begun setting by the time Green, Lawrence, Brooks, and Harmon were able to take their lunch break that evening. Three a.m. lunch breaks were one of the things Green had got the hang of, since that was when the munchies and caffeine crash tended to set in, and nothing scratched that itch quite like greasy meats and burnt coffee.

Officer Lawrence paused in the middle of chewing his burger and shut his eyes. As Green looked around the table, Harmon and Brooks were doing the same.

That could only mean one thing: dispatch was sending out a new call.

When the other officers opened their eyes, Green asked, "What's the deal?"

Brooks answered. "Same old. Some poor person has done fucked up and entered a rich neighborhood; naturally, it's time for the cops to clean up this tragedy." She took a big bite of her burger and then leaned to the side, pulled some cash from her back pocket and threw it on the table of the all-night diner. "Don't hurt yourself rushing to it, gentlemen," she added sarcastically. "Let the lady handle this."

"I don't know if I'd call you *that*," Lawrence said. "I've seen your pat-downs. No lady gets in the nooks and crannies like you do." He threw down some cash, too. "I'll come with."

"Well, aren't you just a knight in shining armor, Lawrence," Officer Harmon grumbled. "Have fun on your quest. I'm gonna stay here and eat my meal with Green. I think fourteen years on patrol in this hellhole of a sector has earned me that."

"I'm actually done," Green said, grimacing apologetically. Not that he didn't appreciate Harmon's presence and experience on calls, but the last thing his stomach needed at the moment was to sit through one of Harmon's intense yet meandering sermons. "I'd better go check my HAM."

Harmon shrugged. "Suit yourself. I was giving you an out, Rookie."

"Not everyone wants to be a lazy-ass, Harmon," Brooks said, scooting out of the booth next to Green.

"But there's one on every shift," Harmon replied. "If not me, then who? I'm just taking one for the team."

Lawrence rolled his eyes. "Such a martyr."

"Nothing wrong with martyrs," Harmon shot back. "In fact, I could tell you a story about one that might change your life."

Lawrence groaned. "Not today, please. I don't think I can take your preaching."

Harmon wasn't deterred. "Some might even call it the greatest story ever told. It's the harrowing tale of our lord and savior." He turned to Green. "You might've heard of him before." He winked. "A man by the name of Count Dracula?"

Green quickly scooted out of the booth, away from the zealous werewolf. "Like I said, gotta go check the HAM."

By the time Green got settled in the driver's seat and pulled up the call list, he was already regretting leaving the comfortable diner, even if it did mean subjecting himself to another one of Officer Harmon's attempts at conversion. But it wouldn't do to hang out and relax while he was the rookie. He'd heard the way officers from other shifts talked about rookies who didn't try to burn themselves out within the first year, and it wasn't anything Green wanted attached to his reputation.

But the call list was empty. None outstanding. Well, he supposed it was a Monday night. He looked at the clock.

Tuesday morning.

People in Fang sector didn't start shooting at each other in earnest until Thursday, usually. Wednesday if it was warm out. The weather lately had been mild, but would that counteract the full moon? The last full moon he'd worked, while he was still with Valance, had been a shitshow of shots fired and maulings.

But even with the full moon, things were fairly calm, and Green found himself unsure what to do next. He supposed he could catch up on some reports until another call came out.

He'd just pulled up the reports on his screen when an alert flashed across it for a new hotshot call.

Armed robbery, suspect fled on foot, 300 block of Weston Estates Blvd. Suspect likely shifter or were-beast.

Weston Estates? What was with the rich neighborhoods tonight?

Green assigned to the call, started his car, and headed to the small sliver of luxury homes in the sector.

It was only a five-minute drive from the diner, and as he pulled off the main road, heading toward Weston Estates Blvd, he checked the HAM to see if anyone else had assigned to the call, too.

Looked like Harmon wasn't so lazy after all. He was already on the way to the victim's home. Did that mean Green wouldn't have to take the report?

Yeah, right.

There was no way a veteran like Harmon would do it himself when he could drop it on the rookie instead.

Then another call sign appeared on the screen under Harmon's.

F701 - in search of suspect

Damn. Valance. He was starting to enjoy not having Valance's piercing blue eyes fixed on him like she knew he was only seconds away from screwing up big time. Hopefully, they could find the suspect soon so *he* could be her punching bag instead of Green.

"Fang 9-01 to Fang 9-07. I'm ten minutes out," came Valance's voice over the radio. "Don't do anything stupid until I get there."

Damn. If she was willing to risk getting reprimanded for talking like that over the radio, she must be more pissed than he'd thought. But then again, Valance tended only to get a slap on the wrist for behavior that would leave other officers suspended or fired. He suspected the higher ups were scared to discipline her for more reasons than just because of who her family was.

Green grunted but didn't respond.

Then she added, "1 to 7, don't do anything stupid once I'm there, either. I know it'll be a struggle for you. Just do your best."

He pulled onto Weston Estates and saw Harmon's car parked in front of the victim's house. He slow-rolled past, deciding where to park when Harmon's voice came over the radio. "Fang 9-05 to Fang 9-07. Robbery sounds legit. Victim claims suspect is armed and on foot. ID-ed as a white male, suspected shifter or were, wearing baggy black pants and a gray tee."

"07 to 05. If you're good with the vic, I'll hunt for the suspect."

"All good here, 7."

Green pulled out from his place by the curb, kept his lights off, and began prowling the streets for any signs of movement.

Considering it'd been about five minutes since the call came in, the radius in which the suspect could be was quite large, especially if he could shift. The odds of Green finding him were slim, but he had to try anyway.

Over the radio, Lawrence piped up. "Fang 9-13 to 9-07, I think we might be looking for the same guy."

"Copy, 9-13. But why do you say that?" Green responded.

"Check your monitor, 7."

Green did, and a third call had come out from the same neighborhood, reporting a suspect who matched the physical description of Green's call, waving a gun around over toward the edge of the neighborhood, near where it transitioned into a high-end shopping mall.

"7 to 13, I'm clear," Green said, "Heading over there now."

"13 to 7, right behind you with 9-02 in tow."

"9-01 is en route, too," Green added more as a warning than reassurance, "but she's a few minutes out."

Green drove past the last reported location and then made his way back, hoping to corral the suspect and box him in.

He was just about to call it off when he saw something large duck behind a tree as he approached one of the front yards to a house that backed up to the road that ran between the neighborhood and the shopping center.

"Fang 9-07 to 9-13. I may have eyes on the suspect," Green radioed. He slowed the car to a crawl as he drove by the tree.

Maybe it was just a shadow that played a trick on his eyes and not a person after all.

Then—nope. A man sprinted out from behind the tree in the direction of the neighborhood. "Shit! Oh fuck. Shit!" Green hollered. He grabbed his radio. "7 to 13, definitely our guy. One running! Corner of Brigsby and Halloway, heading north down Brigsby away from the shopping center."

By the time he'd finished giving his location, he was already out of the car, his feet carrying him in pursuit without direct orders from his brain.

They ran the long block quickly, passing manicured lawns until the suspect rounded the corner of the house at the end of the street. Green called it out to the others. "Turned right. Fleeing east down Farris Heath."

Sergeant Montoya's voice crackled over the radio. "Fang 9-90 to 9-07. Proceed with caution. All units back up to Halloway and Diana's Pass. Officer in pursuit, hold the air."

After a momentary lapse, Green caught sight of the suspect again when the man stutter-stepped to grab at his pants and keep them from falling. "Police!" Green yelled, as if the guy didn't already know that. "Stop! Get on the ground!"

Unsurprisingly, the suspect didn't listen. Instead, he took another right on Diana's Pass, heading back toward Halloway.

God, I hope I don't have to chase this guy in a circle all night.

Green radioed the new location and felt relief pulse through his tired legs when Lawrence responded with,

"Clear. He's heading back toward us. We're setting up now, and we'll flank him as he approaches and box him in."

Green was catching up, slowly but surely, though he maintained as much distance as he could while keeping the suspect in his sights. Luckily the man hadn't shifted. Yet, at least. Maybe the adrenaline of the chase had kept the suspect from thinking of the obvious solution to evading arrest, but if it was a shifter, it might not be much longer before his fight or flight response caused him to do so literally.

As Green crested a hill, he saw the glint of Lawrence's and Brooks's cars parked at the intersection of Diana's Pass and Halloway, creating more of a mental barricade than a physical one—Green knew both vehicles were empty; the suspect did not. From fifty feet away and with the windows rolled up, there was no way the suspect could see past the reflection of streetlights and the full moon to tell that the driver's seats of each car were vacant.

The suspect stopped in his tracks. His head swiveled around, looking to run left or right, but those options were ruled out when Lawrence stepped out from the shadow of a thick oak tree, gun drawn, flanking the suspect from left, and Brooks stepped out from behind an SUV on the right, her firearm extended, too.

"Get on the ground!" Brooks shouted. "Try to shift, and we'll be forced to shoot!"

The suspect's arms flew up into the air as he slowly turned to face Green.

It was the closest thing to supernatural powers Green had ever experienced. He was aware of so many things at once. The slight breeze on his face, the suspect's dilated pupils, Lawrence's and Brooks's measured movements as they side-stepped closer to Green, keeping a safe distance from the suspect. Green kept his mind attuned to any slight twitch of the suspect's muscles that might indicate the start of a shift.

"On the ground! Hands behind your head!" Lawrence shouted.

The man nodded, slowly kneeling down in the street, his hands clasped together behind his head. One knee, then the other …

But he didn't go all the way down. "I didn't do nothin'! I don't even know why you're chasing me!" His hands came unclasped, but he kept them in the air.

"Behind your head!" Brooks shouted. "Face down! Now!"

He ignored the command. "Please officers, I ain't done nothin'!"

"Get the fuck on the ground!" Lawrence shouted.

The man became frantic. "Don't shoot me!" He raised his hands straight up, and his shirt lifted just enough for Green to catch the glint of metal tucked into the man's waistband.

"Gun!" Green called.

"Do what we say, and we don't shoot," Brooks shouted. "Hands behind your head and face down on the ground! Now!"

When the man still didn't fully comply, Green felt an alarm trigger in his mind. This was taking too long. They were giving an armed man too much time to think. It was time to put an end to this.

He glanced at Lawrence, who nodded, side stepped away and provided lethal coverage.

With the suspect's attention focused mostly on Brooks,

Green rushed forward to get cuffs on this man and disarm him as quickly as possible.

But he only made it a few steps before everything changed in a split second.

The suspect lowered his hands toward his head but didn't stop there.

"Don't move!" Green shouted.

The man was an idiot, but was he suicidal? Green's disbelief cost him a split second of hesitation.

Did Brooks tell the man to freeze? Did Lawrence? Nothing quite registered except the pop of a bullet from the suspect's gun that he aimed it at the closest target: Officer Brooks.

Dread flooded Green's veins. Had he hesitated a thousandth of a second too long?

That rush of adrenaline flowed through his arms and numbed his mind as he planted his feet and opened fire at the suspect with his .40.

Green shot to kill. It was instinct, one he didn't know lay dormant inside him, and for how long? Perhaps it dated back to long before the academy. There was no trick shooting the suspect's gun; there was no shooting to injure until the suspect gave up; that fluff was for the movies.

Each tool on his belt had a single purpose—to contain, to cripple—and his gun was no different. If he was threatened with lethal force, it wasn't meant to wing or stun or temporarily incapacitate. Its only purpose was to kill, and he would use as many bullets as it took. Because once that line was crossed, the objective exposed and raw, what harm were eleven more rounds? Deadly force was deadly force.

The first fruitless click of the empty magazine felt like a bucket of ice water to Green's face, and he regained himself, the gun soldered to his hands now, an extension of his body from here on out. Everything was heightened. Had he been the only one shooting? He thought he'd heard more.

"Stop shooting!" he shouted, although the other officers had already done so by then.

Green approached the suspect quickly but cautiously, his shaky fingers fumbling with the spare magazine as he attempted to reload. But then he felt the magazine strike gold and extended his gun out in front of him.

"You good?" shouted Officer Lawrence, rushing up to his side.

Green didn't dare lift his finger from his pistol for a second, not even to give a thumbs-up. He nodded exaggeratedly instead. "Yeah, you?"

"All good," Lawrence replied, close on his right now. "Brooks, you good?"

"Yeah, I'm good," she replied. "Weapon's secure."

As he bent down toward the suspect, the smell of evacuated bowels alone should have told him all he needed to know, but he had to be sure, not just for his peace of mind, but because procedure called for it. This situation was fucked enough without him piling policy violations onto the heap.

There was an alarming lack of blood for how many bullet holes were immediately visible. The odd detail lodged itself into Green's mind, even as he reached in his belt for his gloves.

But before he could successfully slip them onto his sweaty fingers, a firm hand on his shoulder caused him to turn. He stared into the clear blue eyes of Officer Heather Valance. Never in his life had he thought he would be relieved to see his nightmare of a former field training officer in all her terrifyingly intense glory.

"Oh hell," Brooks said from somewhere behind Valance, "looks like I'm shot."

As his worst fears bubbled to the surface of his mind, he leaned to the side to see past Valance.

The suspect's gun dangled in one of her hands, and she looked down at her leg like maybe someone had splashed a little mud on it. "I think I'm OK." She looked up and waved off the other officers. "Just nicked me."

As Officer Lawrence rushed over to her anyway, Valance grabbed Green's shoulders and shook him gently. "Take a deep breath, Officer. Think. What's first?"

He struggled to turn his brain on again. It seemed to have ducked for cover the moment the suspect fired, allowing instinct and training to take over.

He swallowed. "Cuffs." She nodded and let go of his shoulders so he could proceed.

But when he reached down for his silvers, she added, "No point. Irons instead."

Not a good sign. But Green clicked on the iron cuffs anyway before rolling the suspect first to one side to check for more weapons, then over onto his back. The man was dead weight. Green hoped not literally.

Valance placed two ungloved fingers on the suspect's neck, but her calm face already seemed resigned to a particular outcome. She nodded then looked up at Green, and her icy eyes urged him to pay attention. "It was a good shoot. You know it, I know it, and every other officer here knows it. Got that?"

Green swallowed and nodded.

"Let's get this done. Check his pulse."

"Gloves?" Green asked.

"Sure. Fine."

Green slipped one on and checked for a pulse. The suspect seemed very dead. "Nothing," Green croaked.

Valance sighed. "We're not calling it yet. Let the paramedics do that whenever they get their ass over here. What next?"

Green nodded. "Chest compressions." The rhythmic pumping of the dead man's ribs felt almost Zen amidst the commotion of his fellow officers scrambling to secure the scene and radio out updates. He almost didn't want to stop, even though he knew it was a lost cause. Valance stayed by his side as he continued the futile attempt. At least internal investigations couldn't say he hadn't tried. But Valance probably knew that, which was why she walked him through it and made sure he didn't quit.

When Valance left him, he felt panic rising, but he continued the compressions. It was the only thing he knew to do.

She returned a moment later with gauze and began packing the suspect's wounds. The bleeding had started to slow noticeably, though. Green felt the first wave of exhaustion wash over him a moment before Valance placed a hand on his back, saying, "Green, paramedics are here."

"Huh?" He looked up to see two serious-faced paramedics staring down at him. "Oh." He jumped up to clear the way and stumbled a few steps back, his eyes still glued to the body. "Why didn't he change back?" he asked.

His former FTO didn't answer him, instead leading him toward Officer Brooks's car further down the street from the scene.

Officer Lawrence met them halfway, and Green was

vaguely aware that he was being handed off from one babysitter to another.

Didn't matter. Maybe Lawrence would answer his question. "Why didn't he change back?"

Jeremy Lawrence had a blood smear along his handsome, defined jawline, and his usual confident smirk was nowhere to be found. "'Cause he's not a shifter or a were, Green."

Fuck. "What is he?"

"Damn, Green." Lawrence rubbed his hand over his chin, unknowingly smearing the blood around, as he led Green down to the car where Brooks was already being bandaged up by another paramedic. "Thought you'd at least recognize your own kind. That stupid son of a bitch is a human."

"I shot a—? I *killed* another human?"

"Assuming the paramedics call it, yeah. Looks like it," Officer Lawrence added unhelpfully. "If it makes you feel any better, it wasn't just you. Brooks and I got a few rounds in." Lawrence grimaced. "It was a good shoot, Green, alright?"

Officer Green nodded but struggled to breathe with any regularity as he turned to look back at the body.

Lawrence grabbed him and turned him back around, giving him a gentle shove down the hill.

He'd shot a human. He'd *killed* a human. Did it matter that Green was a human, too? *Probably not. Shit.*

Only two months on the job and Green had already screwed his career. Forget about the way people back home were going to treat him now that he'd killed one of his own. Was his whole life fucked because this dumb sieve of a man lying on the ground in front of him just *had* to draw a gun?

His heart pumped rapidly somewhere near his ears as

the first glimmer of sunlight peeked in the east, and he suspected this would be the longest morning of his very brief career.

When he reached Brooks's car at the bottom of the hill, he turned and leaned his back against it, looking at the practiced scene unfold: the supervisors arriving, calm as could be; the paramedics completing their due diligence on the dead victim, clearly just going through the motions at this point; plain-clothes detectives searching for bullet casings in the streets and manicured lawns like children on an Easter egg hunt.

The paramedic finished attending to Aliyah's leg and hurried off to no doubt glimpse at the more exciting wounds of the suspect, leaving Green and her alone.

"Did you shoot?" Green asked, feeling lightheaded.

"Yeah. Yeah, I did. But we're technically not supposed to talk about it from here on out." She rose, grimacing subtly, and moved to stand in front of him, blocking his line of sight to the murder scene so that he had to focus on her face instead. Despite looking as tired as he felt, her slender, mocha-colored face maintained its simple, straightforward beauty. "It's gonna be a long morning, Norman. Pace yourself. I suggest ya get the events firm in your mind while they're still fresh. Write 'em down if you can manage."

"Have you ever shot anyone before?"

Brooks inhaled deeply through her nose, out through her mouth, turning to lean up against the car, shoulder to shoulder with him now. "Not on this job. But yeah. In South America."

"You were in South America, too?"

She nodded, exhaustion clearly settling into her spine. "Rookie, *everyone* was in South America. Or at least

218

everyone who didn't qualify for the human exemption." She patted him on the knee and stood. "We'll have plenty of time to discuss it while we're on paid admin leave. I better check on Lawrence. He mighta messed up his hair in the ruckus, and you *know* how that handsome bitch gets about his hair. Take care of yourself and get ready for what comes next. And remember, it was a good shoot." She pointed at her bandaged calf. "Whatever you do, don't let yourself start to doubt it."

She walked off, leaving Green alone as the dust settled in his mind. He stared up at the sky to take his eyes off the disconcertingly calm scene.

Goddamn full moon.

Maybe it was a good shoot, but he'd murdered a man all the same. The one thing everyone had warned him not to do before the board evaluation was finalized, he'd managed to go and do. Would it even matter whether it was a good shoot if the Kilhaven Police Department decided he was a liability and fired him immediately? Would that hurt his chances of avoiding indictment? Without the uniform to back him up, would he just be seen as a regular old murderer? Would he spend his life in jail?

It was a good shoot.

But how much did that matter? It was a philosophical question he didn't have the energy to resolve tonight, that was for sure. He decided to take Brooks's advice and just focus on preparing for what came next.

Only one problem: Green had no fucking clue what came next.

———

"Man, glad I passed on that bump of cocaine the other night," Lawrence joked as the hospital nurse drew a vial of his blood.

It was standard procedure for an officer's blood to be drawn after firing his or her weapon. The department had to cover its ass in the event of a juiced-up case of 'roid rage getting too trigger happy on duty.

Green had never done an illegal drug in his life, yet still, he couldn't help but feel nervous about it. What if someone had slipped something in his drink? What if he ate a bunch of poppy seed bagels and just didn't remember?

Okay, maybe the adrenaline was messing with his brain because he'd never eaten a poppy seed bagel in his life.

"Doing okay, Green?" Brooks asked, leaning forward in her chair to see past Lawrence.

"Me? I'm fine. How are *you* doing?" He nodded at her bandaged calf where the bullet had grazed her.

She held up her leg and stared down at it. "Meh, it's fine. Kinda smarts now that the adrenaline's worn off, but I'll just shift when I get home, and it'll heal up quick. Plus, we probably got a month of leave to recover while the department does its due diligence."

"If we're lucky it'll only be a month," Lawrence said. "Garrison over in Claw sector was out for five months while they investigated his shooting."

Brooks sucked in air. "Oof ... that's a lot of lost overtime pay." The nurse taking her blood slipped out the needle and wandered off with five vials of blood. "But that won't be the case here. Don't get much more clear cut than three officers firing at once."

Lawrence chuckled morosely. "Right. We'll see." He leaned his head back against the chair, shutting his eyes, clearly as tired as Green after a long morning and a longer afternoon. "Maybe I'll go hunting," Lawrence said. "I haven't been on a hunting trip in a while. I spend so much damn time at work; I almost never have time to shift. Might feel good get out of my head for a while."

"Amen to that," Brooks said. "My panther's been clawing at me since that foot pursuit a couple weeks ago." She glanced over at Green. "Wait, you got a way to unwind?"

"Uhh …" He thought about it. Then his mind landed on one surefire way. "Yeah."

Lawrence cracked open an eye and rolled his head toward Green. "And that is?"

Green shrugged, then flinched when the gesture jiggled the needle in his arm. "Women. Well, woman. Singular."

Lawrence grinned sleepily. "Oh yeah? You got yourself a woman, Green? You gotta tell me how you did it when you're working nightshift. I still haven't managed to figure that one out."

Before Green could respond, Brooks said, "It's someone he sees at work, that's how he does it."

Lawrence's eyes shot open. "Huh? Who?"

Green wished, not for the first time, that he was a telepath so he could send Brooks a quick message to shut the hell up. If she knew, that was bad enough, but he didn't need the whole shift knowing, which is what would happen if Lawrence heard about it. Men as good looking as Lawrence always hated it when someone less attractive could get a woman.

But he didn't have any telepathic abilities and had to settle for staring at Brooks with a stern warning in his eyes.

It didn't work.

"Hellstrom," Brooks said, hitching a brow Green's

serious expression and clearly not caring. "He's been banging Hellstrom."

Lawrence's jaw dropped, and his head spun around toward Green. Then a moment later, he guffawed. "Oh, you poor bastard! Man, oh man. Hellstrom … You boned yourself on that one, Green. She's her very own kind of jailbait."

"Oh hush," Green said, too exhausted to say anything more forceful. "She's not what everyone says she is."

"No," Lawrence replied, "she's exactly what everyone says she is, assuming everyone says she's a shriveled—"

"Taint, I know," Green finished.

Lawrence cocked his head to the side. "Nooo … wasn't going to say taint." He squinted at Green, disgust turning down the corners of his mouth. "Really, Green? A shriveled taint? That's filthy. No, I was going to say a shriveled hag."

"That's an insult to hags," Brooks said.

Green opened his mouth to say they were both wrong, but that wasn't much of a counterargument. These two weren't going to be persuaded. But the Becky they knew wasn't the Becky he knew. And he knew her pretty well, he thought. "Okay, I'll play along. Why do you think she's a shriveled—Why don't you like her?"

Lawrence and Brooks shared a pitying glance and Brooks said, "He asked. Ya might as well tell him."

Nodding, Lawrence turned back toward him and frowned apologetically. "I almost feel bad telling you, since it sort of strips you of your piece of ass that you'll sorely need while on admin leave, but whatever. I'd hate to see you go the way of Detective Freemont."

"*Former* Detective Freemont," Brooks added.

Trying to follow along, Green shook his head slightly. "Who's that?"

Lawrence said, "Former lover of Becky Hellstrom."

And Brooks added, "Ex-husband of Heather Valance."

Green previously thought his energy had bottomed out, but apparently, there'd still been a little something left in the tank—and now it was gone. His head spun. "Wait."

"Yep." Brooks nodded.

Well, this blew a big one. "But how do you know?"

"Telepaths can send words, *and* they can send pictures," Lawrence responded. "When Freemont got scared that Valance would find out about the cheating, he tried to break it off. And then Hellstrom sent pictures."

Brooks leaned forward. "To. Everyone."

"Well, first to Valance. And then to everyone."

Green shook his head. "No, that can't be true. She wouldn't do that."

Lawrence placed a firm hand on Green's shoulder. "And I'm telling you it *is* true. Because she sent the images to me. Really nasty stuff, too. I mean, if that was the kind of shit Detective Freemont was into, I get that Valance wouldn't participate in it. But damn. For him to go find someone else. Cold. And a telepath? Just fucking stupid."

"Welcome to the world of dating men," Brooks said bitterly. "But yeah, Hellstrom sent me the images—well, more like video highlights—too."

He knew he was grasping at straws here, but he grasped at them anyway. "Just because she sent you images doesn't mean it happened, though, right? I mean, couldn't she have just imaged up a scenario and then sent it out to piss off Valance?"

Brooks held up a hand to stop him. "Okay, first of all, no.

There's an obvious difference between images telepaths have witnessed and ones they've just imagined. The latter has a lot of little wiggly shit around the outside edges. But more importantly, even if Hellstrom *had* made up those images, would sending them around to everyone on the shift to convince people she'd fucked Valance's husband in a lot of weird, furry ways make her something other than a shriveled taint?" She held up her hands defensively. "Your words, not mine."

Damn. Brooks had a point. "She sent them to everyone on the shift?" God, this was awful.

Lawrence nodded. "Yep. Took quite a bit of convincing to keep Valance from transferring out. But she knows we got her back now."

Brooks nodded. "Exactly. The other day, I managed to slip a dead cockroach into the bag of chips Hellstrom was munching on while she wasn't looking. Point is, we look out for each other on the Fang 900s. And that's why you need to listen to us when we say you should leave Hellstrom at a desert truck stop and never look back, figuratively speaking."

Lawrence leaned in conspiratorially. "Or literally speaking, if you think you can pull it off without getting caught."

When Green sighed and leaned back in his chair, flinching only slightly as the nurse pulled out his needle, Brooks reached over Lawrence and rested a comforting hand on Green's knee. "Sorry to be the one to tell ya all this."

Lawrence pushed her arm out from across his lap. "No, you're not. You love it."

She leaned back. "Yeah, that's true. I shoulda said something sooner."

Keeping his eyes open was a struggle at this point. *Jesus, how much blood did they take from me?* All he wanted was to go home, crawl into bed, and sleep for a day or so. Except he suspected that once he was well rested, that was when the trauma of just having riddled a human with bullet holes would rear its ugly head in earnest.

And then there was the fallout that would surely come from Bowers.

No, don't think about that yet.

"Well, I'm still not entirely convinced," he said. "No offense. I mean, I believe that you believe that story, but until I talk to Becky, I don't want to jump to conclusions."

Brooks held up her hands in resignation. "Fine, I get that. Just know that whenever you realize we're one hundred percent right and have been the whole time, we won't fault ya for it, so just come right out and admit it."

"Yeah," Lawrence added, "I was all ready to saddle up that banshee and ride her myself until I was forced to hate her. I get it, man. And hey, you're about to have plenty of leave to find some other sweet thing to take your mind off work. So there's that."

"There's that," Green echoed gloomily.

He'd give Becky a chance to defend the claims, sure, but things just weren't looking good. Dread filled his gut at the prospect of confronting her. Was that because he felt bad accusing her of something she would never do? Or was it because he already knew what she'd say and just didn't want to hear it?

He'd find out soon enough.

CHAPTER TWENTY_

When a loud knocking pulled him out of a weighty but restless sleep, Green couldn't have guessed what day of the week it was if someone had pointed a gun at his head. A small bit of light crept in between his black-out curtains, but that didn't necessarily mean it was light outside; his bedroom window was right next to the security light on the building, so it never got fully dark.

What day had he killed a man? Tuesday? It seemed like maybe it was a Tuesday. But it was technically in the morning. Did that make it Wednesday? Or was it Monday night leading into Tuesday morning? Tuesday seemed like a weird day to kill a human; maybe it wasn't a Tuesday. Either way, it was no help in figuring out what the fuck day it was now. Or what the fuck night.

The knocking persisted, louder this time. Green crawled out of bed, too tired to cover the casual erection that tented his navy blue briefs.

Ambling stiffly to the door, he peeped through the hole to see Becky standing outside. She looked pissed. He breathed in deeply, stared sorrowfully at his dick—now probably wasn't the time—and then massaged it down before opening the door.

"Why aren't you answering my calls?" She stormed past him into the apartment before he could respond.

He turned around, and she was already bracing herself in the doorway of the kitchen with her fists on her hips. "You're involved in a shooting, and I have to hear about it through the grapevine, and then when I call you to make sure you're okay, you ignore my calls for almost twenty-four hours?" She lifted her eyebrows, waiting for a response.

"Wait, what time is it?"

Wrong question, it seemed. "That's all you have to say? 'What time is it?' What the hell, Norman!"

A few avant-garde garbage images from his dreams clunked around his head as he tried to get his feet under him with this Becky situation. "What should I have done? I was in the hospital and then dealing with paperwork and commanding officers and recording statements for hours afterward. They didn't let me talk to anyone, and then once I got home I just crashed, and then … well, I guess this is the first I've been up since then. I don't even know what day it is."

"I just thought what we had was something a little more substantial than how you see it, apparently. If I were in your shoes, I'd have called you right away." Her eyes grew watery, and her chin quivered slightly. "I guess I've just been wrong. I guess I've just let myself be used by yet another man." When the first tear ran down her cheek, Green realized he had no impulse to wipe it away for her.

She walked past him again and through the open door, but paused just outside the threshold. "Have I misjudged you, Norman? Tell me I'm wrong, that you love me and want me in your life, and I'll stay."

He took her in, all of her, all her curves and tight clothing and *oh-holy-hell* cleavage. He imagined pressing his fingertips into the softness above her hips, driving himself into her and the glorious feel of her warmth.

It was a real shame that sweet, giving body was probably inhabited by a psycho. "Tell me something," he said.

His cool tone seemed to catch her off guard, incongruous as it was with her melodrama. "Yes?"

"Did you fuck Detective Freemont and then send mental pictures of it to all of the Fang 900s?"

The waterworks stopped, as if someone had flipped an emergency shut-off switch. She chuckled dryly. "Well, it's been a good run, Green. And yes, I did that. But only because she didn't give him what he needed."

Green was relieved to discover a lack of emotion on his end regarding this result. He felt detached, separate, and hopefully not in a way that would require attention during his mandatory therapy meetings during his admin leave. "I heard you two did some pretty fucked up shit together."

She rolled her eyes. "You *would* think that, with your boring human positions and quick trigger."

Green stepped toward her so that he stood only two feet away. He looked her in the eyes. "Yeah, I guess you really are a shriveled taint." And before she could say anything else, he slammed the door and went back to bed.

He'd need all the sleep he could get if he was going to muster the courage to admit to Valance that he'd been wrong about Hellstrom the whole time.

CHAPTER TWENTY-ONE_

I should probably take out the recycling.

Green stared down at the heaping pile of beer bottles, beer cans, and cardboard microwave dinner boxes before admitting there was a more pressing matter.

I should probably take out the trash.

That meant putting on pants. Well, he had to do it sometime, he supposed. He couldn't spend the entirety of his admin leave without pants on.

Or could he?

No, he couldn't. That garbage smelled like shit.

He pulled on a pair of basketball shorts, bagged the trash and the recycling, and took it downstairs to the Dumpsters. By the time he returned, he was slightly winded. That probably had to do with the fact that he'd eaten almost nothing in the past week since the shooting, and he'd exercised even less. He grabbed a slightly freezer-burned breakfast sandwich and threw it into the microwave on a paper towel before plopping down at the table, opening his slow-as-dirt laptop, and seeing how long he could distract himself before he inevitably turned to porn for some mental relief.

Reading the news was no good, but he did it anyway. A masochistic obsession had developed in him where he devoured every piece of coverage about his shooting that he could find, trying to rate it on a scale of one to ten, one being complete bullshit and ten being how he remembered it. Nothing had yet scored above a three.

After grabbing his scalding, soggy sandwich from the microwave, he returned to the table just as his phone rang on the counter. Meh, too far to reach sitting down, and it was probably just someone from Bowers calling to scream at him again. That had happened twice already. He didn't even remember going to school with the second guy, though that dude sure was adamant that they were old friends and therefore the betrayal of Green's own kind stung all the more because of it.

His mother had called, too. She didn't blame him, but she found a way to talk about her feelings more than Green could stomach, and he'd hung up on her. That would bite him in the ass for sure, but it could get in the back of the long line of things that were sure to bite him in the ass. He would have no ass left within a year. He was sure about that, too.

He gave in a pulled up some porn. It wasn't particularly good. There were two men coercing consent from a woman, which was generally in line with Green's voyeuristic preferences, but the framing was a little canted, and it quickly grated on Green's nerves. How incompetent could these pornographers be that they didn't even check the shot before going at it? Goddamn amateurs.

Oh God, what if it's intentional? What if they did that to be ... what, artistic?

He didn't want freaking arthouse porn. He just wanted a few people boning with the goddamn camera horizontal to the goddamn floor! He let go of himself, slipped his hand out of his boxer-briefs, and slammed the laptop shut before the woman on screen even got to the obligatory "I've never done anything like this before." Then he stood up from the table in a hurry.

He stuffed his mouth with another hunk of the soggy breakfast sandwich and scanned the apartment. How had he let it get this messy? He didn't even know he had this many things. Someone ransacking the place couldn't have left so much scattered around.

He needed to clean.

But that seemed like a big deal. And he was still so tired.

Well, Rome wasn't built in a day.

He grabbed some air freshener from below the sink, sprayed it around the living room and dining room, and called it good.

A knock on the front door sent panic through his chest, and he instinctively looked around for a place to hide.

Then his brain began to ask the right questions.

Who is it?

Is it Hellstrom?

Oh, God. Is it Mom?

Do people ever stop fearing that it's their mother knocking at the door?

There was only one intelligent way to approach this, and that was to pretend he wasn't home.

Then another hard knock was followed by, "Green, I

know you're in there. I can smell you." And Green realized that it was neither his mother nor Hellstrom.

It was someone more fearsome.

But unlike his mother and Hellstrom, there wasn't a snowball's chance in hell Valance would give up and walk away. More likely she would break down his door and find some genius way to articulate it so that she never faced repercussions and he was left reimbursing the apartment complex for a replacement frame.

When he opened it, what he found made so little sense with everything his brain knew to be true, he was struck with an impulse to laugh that managed to rival his impulse to flee.

Officer Valance was out of uniform.

Her brown hair was free from the usual confines of a tight bun and a thick layer of hairspray to hold it down, instead cascading over her shoulders in loose waves. *How hair should be,* Green thought, dumbfounded.

A casual gray, crew-neck T-shirt and dark-wash jeans completed her off-duty look. And while it was anything but fancy, it was so vastly different from everything he associated with her that he wondered briefly if she had a sister—maybe one younger than her by a few years—who she'd sent over to check on him.

But when he met her ice-blue eyes, noticed the way they stared at him like he might be a little slow and even if he'd been born that way she had zero sympathy for it, he knew it was his former FTO standing before him. Then she spoke, and it was confirmed.

"Smells like you're hard-boiling turds in Febreze. Is now a bad time?"

"You're not still pissed at me?"

232

"Pissed? No. I pity you—for a lot of reasons—but I don't hold grudges."

He didn't believe that for a second.

She pushed past him, and as he turned, he saw that she carried a brown duffle bag over her shoulder.

"What's that?"

She paused at the kitchen table, scanned for a clean spot, then gave up and pushed some of the junk into the middle to clear a space for the bag. "Homework." She reached for the zipper then paused and scented the air before her eyes landed on Green, judgment and disapproval clear in them. It didn't take a genius to figure out what she was smelling.

"She hasn't been here in a week. We broke up."

"You realized she was an old shriveled taint." Not a question.

Green nodded. "Yeah, I figured that out. Sorry it took so long."

A tiny smirk turned the corner of her mouth, and she shrugged a shoulder. "Don't worry about it. Nobody claims you're the boy genius of the shift." She unzipped the bag but didn't open it right away. "Are you good? Or do you want to talk about your feelings and maybe ask me if I think Hellstrom is banging someone else? Because the answer to that is 'I've never been more certain of anything in my life.' If I'm honest, and this may come as a bit of a surprise to you, I would rather watch Hellstrom swoop down on my ex-husband while he slept and steal sperm from his limp dick like the succubus she is than talk about your feelings on the breakup."

Green nodded. Valance was doing more for his alertness than the entire pot of coffee he'd consumed a few hours earlier had. "I guess I'm good then."

She nodded. "Damn right you are. But you're not *that* good, which is why I'm here." She pulled open the duffle, and there was no mistaking the evidence bags inside, some of them hardly filled, others near bursting, all of them containing drugs or ... was that hair?

"Jesus, Valance. What the hell is this?"

She pulled out a chair from the table and sat. "Don't look so scared. I signed out everything. Well, most everything. Okay, only a few things. Like the fur."

"It's fur? Not human hair?" That was reassuring for some reason.

"Well, *that's* fur"—she pointed to a bag of short orange strands—"but that"—she pointed to another bag, one that was threatening to pop open from overfill—"yeah, that's human hair."

Green surveyed the bags as she pulled them out one by one and laid them on the table. He had the sudden impulse to move the pair of dirty socks to keep them from becoming contaminated. "Do you mind if I ask why you brought this to my house?"

She sighed and looked up at him. "I mind a little, but only because it's such a dumb question. I brought all this here because if I made you shut your eyes and sniff each of these things—"

"Please don't make me do that."

"—you wouldn't be able to tell one apart from the other. We need to change that. It's time for a little scent training, Rookie."

Green remained standing, his arms folded across his chest as he stared down at the piles. "Doesn't this seem a little pre-emptive? I mean, I don't even know for sure that I passed the board evaluation, and now that I've shot someone ..." He sighed then looked up at her.

She was staring at him like he was stupid. Even more than she usually did. "Green, you passed the ... wait, have you gone all week without knowing?" She chuckled. "Shit. That's sad."

"Wait, what? I passed?"

"Yeah. It was posted online last week. Plus, I outright told you afterward. What did you think I meant by 'you got it'?"

"I thought you were just being supportive!"

She narrowed her eyes at him. "That doesn't sound like me."

Green exhaled and let his shoulders deflate. "God dammit, Valance."

"You don't seem excited."

"Of course I am. But it would've been nice to know a week ago."

"Then you should've checked online."

He shut his eyes to steady himself. Valance was definitely enjoying this more than her calm voice let on, so he tried not to give her the satisfaction of seeing him too wound up. "The department never posts things online. How was I supposed to know to check online?"

"They do post things online for humans. You people love that shit. Now shall we celebrate with a little extra training so that you don't get yourself killed?" She crossed her arms and waited.

"Sure, fine. But I don't know if this is even going to help. I'm still just a human."

"Well duh." She nodded a concession. "But worse

handicaps have been overcome before. Besides, your options are either to give this a shot, or to give up before you try and accept that you'll probably fuck-up in very special ways that results in the death of one of your own kind—or worse—one of *my* kind. And Brooks and Lawrence may not be there next time to help cover your ass." She raised her eyebrows, and while he knew that was supposed to insinuate something, he hadn't the slightest clue as to what. Did she know something he didn't?

Well, she already thought he was an idiot.

"What do you mean 'cover your ass'? I could've handled that guy myself."

But even as he said it, he realized how stupid he sounded.

Valance sighed. "Sure you could. I mean, the odds are against it, but I'm not talking about saving your life, I'm talking about covering your ass so the department didn't hang you out to dry."

"Why would they hang me out to dry?"

Valance shut her mouth and her jaw twitched, a clear sign of growing impatience. "Sit your ass down, Green. It's time for me to spell out a few things for you."

He followed orders then immediately scolded himself for doing it so hurriedly in his own home.

She leaned over the table toward him. "You killed a human. I know you didn't want to or whatever, but you did. Now, judging from the state of your apartment, I assume you've managed to find ways to distract yourself from the new reality of being a killer; namely, wallowing in your filth. But that's just who you are now. You took another man's life. It was a good shoot. Everyone knows that, from Chief Spinner all the way down to you. But it was still a human, and that is *not* what the department wants. And by 'the department' I mean the politicians posing as cops who run the show and have their heads so far up the ass of public perception that they're sucking on its tonsils.

"The point is that if it'd just been you who fired, if there weren't two other cops unloading into that ticking shit-bomb human, you would likely be on permanent unpaid leave, not temporary paid leave."

"But you said it was a good shoot."

"It was. The public doesn't give two shits about that, though. Look at those sheltered assholes up in Crown Tree. They've had the luxury of vacation lives where they can prance around saying no one should ever take the life of another, zero exceptions. They hate anything that points out the obvious—that *someone* has to handle with those who want to take out innocent people for nothing more than shits and giggles.

"Then, those elves start pumping out the bullshit sob stories of the fuckers we take down. They dig up the one photo where the dipshit looks halfway intelligent and is smiling like maybe, just maybe, there's a soul somewhere behind those eyes. And the public slurps that shit up and begs for more.

"It would have been easy for the chief to get on his high horse and say, 'We regret this happening, we're sorry for the family of the victim, blah blah blah, and the officer responsible for the shooting has been terminated, and we're looking into criminal charges.' Spinner would have human rights activists lining up to blow him if he did that, and no one on either side would bother questioning it because it's just *easier* to offer you up as the virgin sacrifice to the gods of public opinion and hope it all goes away.

"But three officers firing, two being on the Force for five

plus years, and one—Brooks—who's received just a fucking upsetting number of awards for valor, is not a situation Spinner can make disappear with a simple scapegoat rookie. No, he has to address it properly, now.

"Ergo, Brooks and Lawrence saved your ass the moment they each pulled the trigger. I wouldn't count on them doing the same for you again."

Green shook his head, hoping it helped his thoughts file into a neat line. "You say that like they shot the guy for me. Pretty sure they fired at him for the same reason I did."

She leaned in closer. "No shit," she said. "But they've done a whole hell of a lot for you since. More than I would do, truth be told." She paused, narrowing her eyes. "You've already submitted your statement, right?"

Green nodded.

"And you have it memorized, right?"

"If reliving it every time I close my eyes counts, then yes."

"Good. Because what I'm about to tell you will fuck that up real good, and I can't have you slipping during your testimony. But also, you need to know something. And I swear to you, if you breathe a word of this, I will—You know what they sometimes do to women about to give birth so that the baby doesn't tear up the mother on its way out?"

Green leaned back. "Uh ... no. I have no clue what they—"

"Well, look up 'episiotomy' later, and know that I'll do that to you, except with B-Rat's rusty hobo shank, if you ever tell anyone you heard this from me."

He was pretty sure he would rather just not hear what she was about to say, but he was too frightened to articulate that. And there was probably nothing he could say that would stop her from proceeding anyway.

"You unloaded into that motherfucker in a way that, truth be told, turned me on a little bit. But an argument could be made—and will be made, by IA nonetheless—that you rushing him escalated the situation unnecessarily."

"But that's bullshit!"

Valance held out a hand, motioning for him to take it down a notch. "But the argument will be made, and you'll have to answer it. Except the other two officers didn't mention it in their statements. Those dumbasses put their careers on the line to save your ass. Because when it comes time for the grand jury, the matching statements of two seasoned officers and war vets in a crisis situation will trump the undoubtedly incoherent and generally poorly written report—no, Green, I've seen your reports so don't even try—of a rookie two weeks off of FTO." She leaned back slightly. "They saved your career, Green. Don't let it go to your oddly shaped head, though; that's just what we do in Fang. Werewolf, shifter, hag, human—doesn't matter. You're one of us now, and we watch out for our own. Because the leadership ain't gonna do it, and the politicians ain't gonna do it, and the public sure as hell ain't gonna do it. And that's why I'm here. I'm trying to save your ass. Now do you have any more stupid questions, or can we get to our scent training?"

"Just one."

She arched a brow at him, impatiently shaking her head. "Yes?"

He blamed poor sleep for what he said next. "You thought it was kinda hot watching me unload into that guy?"

To his surprise, she didn't insult him or physically threaten him in any way. Instead, she pouted out her lips slightly and said, "Yeah, a little bit." Then she grabbed a baggie of fur off the table and held it up to him, holding back a surprisingly girlish grin. "Here, start with this one."

Was she *flirting* with him? Did Valance have the hots for him now? Hell, he was horny. He shouldn't have shut off the porn before the "I've never done this before" line.

Without thinking twice, he held the baggie just beneath his nostrils and inhaled deeply, meeting Valance's uncharacteristically bashful eyes. "What is this?" he asked, then inhaled even more deeply as the grin she'd held back finally surfaced … and wasn't a grin at all, but a smirk.

"Some asshole's fur. And I mean that literally. It's fur from a were-bear asshole."

"Oh, God." He dropped the baggie. "Oh … God." He pushed his chair back from the table. "Oh … GOD! I think I got bits up my nose!" He snorted out as hard as he could.

While he fought against his gag reflex, Valance chuckled. "But now are you ever going to forget that smell? I bet not."

He jumped up and braced himself over the sink, heaving up breakfast sandwich in wet, fruitful bursts. As much as he hated it, he had to admit she had a point. Her methods might not be orthodox or legal or even morally acceptable, but Valance was one hell of a teacher.

"How about that one?" Valance said from the corner of her mouth as another protestor passed close by.

Green inhaled deeply. "Were-beast?"

Valance rolled her eyes. "No shit. But what kind?"

The woman had already passed by, so another sniff wasn't an option. "Baboon?"

Her only outward sign of annoyance was a sharp inhale. Otherwise, she maintained her usual professional demeanor of a scowl, feet spread shoulder width apart, her hands folded loosely together by her duty belt. "Really? Baboon? For fuck's sake, Green, look at her gait."

He did. It didn't help. "Were-chimp?"

Valance's head whirled around to inspect him from head to toe, presumably looking for signs of intelligence as she often did. "Were-chimp? Were-baboon is wrong so your next guess is a very similar kind of wrong? No, Green. There's no such thing as a were-chimp. That was a were-badger."

"Were-badger?! How— I didn't even know that was a thing!"

Valance returned her gaze to the marching protestors. "Calm down, Rookie. And focus. You're supposed to be protecting these people, not acting as irrational as they are."

Green surveyed the crowd, and to the untrained nose, this protest and counter-protest would be a confusing situation indeed. It was impossible to tell just by looking at each person which side they belonged to, the anti-creature coalition or the anti-human front. Or was it pro-creature? He couldn't remember how each group thought of themselves, only the terms in which each group thought of the other, and he only kept *that* straight because it was written on the signs each person carried.

But Green's was no longer an untrained nose. In fact, over the past three months, his nose had endured more intense training than he supposed the rest of him had endured throughout the entire police academy.

Picking up this overtime assignment was just another chapter in Valance's unorthodox textbook, and it was an advanced chapter, too. With so many breeds this close together, he had to focus to take in a solid whiff and rack his scent memory for a name.

"I don't think we even covered were-horse," he continued, keeping his voice calm to avoid another admonishment from his sensei from hell.

"Of course we did." But even she didn't sound certain. "What about this one coming in quick?"

She was clearly trying to change the subject, but Green gave the man a sniff anyway. "Were-bear." He swallowed hard against the bile rising in his throat. "Definitely were-bear."

"You never forget your first," she said, her gaze grazing the tops of the protestor's heads as they passed where she and Green had set up at a barricaded cross street.

It'd been a long, hot afternoon, and while Green was thankful at first for a little bit of sunlight so he didn't die of a nightshift-induced vitamin D deficiency, he quickly regretted the decision of working an eight-hour shift where he was forced to stand on asphalt in full gear.

Just as he was wondering who he had to shoot to get a bottle of water, two voices rose up from not far off in the crowd, toward the center of the flowing mass of people.

Not good.

Valance elbowed him and nodded toward it, but he was already well aware, his senses heightened into the intoxicating and addictive state of alertness he only ever experienced on the job.

Two voices hollering once could just be drunk friends shouting hello. He waited for another yell.

He didn't have to wait long. Valance got a half step on him as they charged into the crowd toward the source of the commotion.

A radius of about three feet had been cleared around the man on the ground as onlookers paused, perhaps caught between the impulse to help and the impulse to gawk and do nothing. The latter was the clear winner.

When one of the anti-human protestors caught sight of Green and Valance, she shouted, "Do something! He needs help!" both of which seemed unnecessary things to tell cops when, firstly, that was clearly why they were there, to do something, and secondly, anyone with eyes, or even just one eye, could see that this man needed help. No one thrashing on the ground like that *didn't* need help in one way or another.

The convulsing man wiggled and jiggled on his side, his back to Valance and Green when they arrived at the edge of the circle, but before they could cross the extra few feet, the man rolled over, and on reflex, Green's right hand reached for the pouch where he kept his gloves. Meanwhile, his mouth, again on reflex, said, "What in God's name is that purple shit coming out of his mouth and nose?"

"And ears," Valance added, sounding less than okay about it herself. "You forgot ears. And I have no idea. But you probably want to make sure none of it gets in *your* mouth, nose, or ears."

He wasn't sure he'd ever agreed with her more fervently.

They knelt down next to the man, with Valance by the convulsing man's side and Green scooting so that his thighs provided something softer than asphalt for the man's head to bang against each time it flung up and then down again.

"Give us space," Valance ordered to the crowd, then she reached for the radio on her shoulder and began calling for backup.

"Oh god, it's coming out of his eyes now," Green said just before a particularly unlucky jerk of the man's head sent a splatter of the purple ooze directly onto Green's cheek. Luckily, he shut his eye in time to keep it from getting in there, but he was pretty sure some made it in his left nostril, and a moment later, the bit above his mouth dripped onto his lips, aided by his sweat from the long, hot day. He turned his head to the side and tried to spit it out, but he could still taste it. It reminded him of the time his mother had made him swig hydrogen peroxide because she'd caught him eating dirt from the garden on a dare.

Except this came from a man's … mouth? Nose? Eyes? Holy hell.

"Stay calm," Valance said, but when he glanced at her, she was clearly shaken. She alternated between staring helplessly down at the seizing man and turning her attention to the crowd, who followed directions to stay back about as well as they expressed a complex political message in the small space afforded by their protest signs, which was to say *not well at all*.

"I got some in my mouth," Green said as calmly as he could. But oops—he'd shouted it, his voice cracking toward the end.

Damn, would this guy just keep convulsing forever? The man's head was delivering a brutal beating to Green's thighs.

Valance looked at him, her piercing eyes focusing on the purple goop clinging to his cheek. "Forget about it. Stay focused, rookie. Nothing you ca—"

Another unfortunate shake of the man's head send loose purple liquid flying in multiple directions, and Green narrowly avoided being hit with it in the face again, instead feeling it land on his neck.

Valance wasn't so lucky, and her words of assurance were cut short when a blob flew directly into her open mouth.

She spat it out. "Oh christ." She spat again. "Oh ball sacks. Why— why does it taste—" She hocked up what she could and spit it onto the asphalt.

All the spitting did what Valance and Green's orders couldn't, moving the crowd back a few more paces. But it didn't do much more than that, at least not for Green, who could still taste the antiseptic acidity in his mouth like it was burning a hole through his tongue. What if that shit was contagious? What if he ended up convulsing on the ground before much longer? What diseases might he have?

Purple streamed from every orifice on the man's face, but all Green could think about was avoiding getting any more of that shit in his body.

Valance pressed her lips together so firmly now they created not much more than a thin white line as she squinted down at the man, trying to play defense against any of his appendages when they made a quick break toward the hard, unforgiving street.

Then the convulsing suddenly stopped, and Green stared down at the man's limp body in front of him.

"Pulse?" Valance asked. Clearly, she didn't want to touch him even though she'd already managed to slip on her gloves.

Fine. That nasty juice was already in his mouth. He could touch the man's slime-covered neck for long enough to check for a pulse.

At first, he felt nothing. Shit. Maybe he had the wrong spot. He thought he felt a slight bit of movement when he slowly moved his fingers toward the center of the man's throat.

He almost had it, but wait, that wasn't like any pulse he'd ever felt.

The man exploded.

Entirely.

For a split second after it happened, even as Green was covered in a thick layer of purple goo and held a shattered skull in his lap, he thought, *maybe that guy* didn't *just explode.* But when he looked at Valance, also covered in a purple sheen and looking much less concerned about the little bit of goop that had found its way into her mouth earlier, it was difficult for him to deny the messy truth of it.

And that was, of course, that yeah, the man had exploded. Sure as shit.

Valance pulled Green to his feet as the crowd ran in all directions—except toward the violet epicenter of the panic. But neither officer could pull their eyes from the remains that splattered across the street before them.

"Okay," Valance said, wiping goo from her mouth and flinging it off to the side. "This is new."

END OF BOOK 1

Turn the page for more from Kilhaven...

Don't stop now.
Start on the next Kilhaven Police book.

More folks explode in this one.
Green gets a little better at his job.
Valance continues to be a scary bitch.
You will love this shit.

www.books2read.com/kilhaven2

HEX TRAFFICKING

Two Kilhaven Police officers pulled over a commercial semi-truck traveling north on FM 293 at 1:30pm last Monday after it was seen careening between lanes. Officers suspected the driver, Margery Roan Huffman, human, 49, of distracted driving and pulled her over to issue her a verbal warning. However, during the verbal interaction, officers report that she began acting erratic and agitated, and they asked her to step out of the truck so the cargo could be searched. At first glance the enclose cargo space appeared empty, but upon closer examination, a false bottom was found. In it were 7,000 hex bags, some of which had broken open during transit.

Huffman was arrested and Stubborn Hauntings Unit agents were called to the scene immediately. Huffman claims she was herself under a hex that could only be lifted if she completed the shipment, but she refused to provide further information as to who might have hexed her or why. She faces up to twenty years in prison for hex trafficking and two counts of hexing a law enforcement officer. Both officers suffered severe boils and unwanted erections as a result of the broken hex bags and are still undergoing testing and treatment by licensed witchcraft professionals.

———

ABOUT THE AUTHORS_

BROCK BLOODWORTH is a private person. He wishes to remain "off the grid" as much as possible. You will not find him on social media, so don't waste your time. If you wish to reach him, consider contacting H. Claire Taylor instead. She's much friendlier.

H. CLAIRE TAYLOR is the author of the Jessica Christ series and deserves a morsel of credit for co-writing the Kilhaven Police series and putting up with Brock's shit. You can learn more about her and her comedy projects at www.hclairetaylor.com.

Find more by Brock and Claire:
www.ffs.media
contact@ffs.media

[f] facebook.com/authorhclairetaylor
[twitter] twitter.com/claireorwhatevs
[BB] bookbub.com/authors/hclairetaylor
[g] goodreads.com/hclairetaylor
[a] amazon.com/author/hclairetaylor

CPSIA information can be obtained
at www.ICGtesting.com
Printed in the USA
BVHW071050170921
616961BV00002B/159

9 781736 728932